GOD OF ANOTHER

THE
SHADOW

Yellow Suit Publishing

CHAD MICHAEL COX

Note: If you purchased this book without a cover, you should be aware that this book is stolen property. It was reported as "unsold and destroyed" to the publisher, and neither the author nor the publisher has received any payment for this "stripped book."

This is a work of fiction. All of the characters, organizations, and events portrayed in this novel are either products of the author's imagination or are used fictitiously.

GOD OF ANOTHER WORLD: THE ADOW

Copyright © 2014 by Chad Michael Cox, LLC

All rights reserved.

Cover Art: Eric Wilkerson
Map Drawing: Ron Wagner

Editors:
Floyd Largent
Tracey Kelley
Nate Granzow

Published by Yellow Suit Publishing
Ankeny, Iowa

www.yellowsuitpublishing.com

ISBN 978-0-9912643-0-8

First Edition: February 2014
Printed in the United States of America

For Jessica—this world would not exist without you;

and to Breanna, Sean, and Heath
who complete my stories.

ACKNOWLEDGEMENTS

I first expressed this story as an idea. I was sitting in a restaurant with a good friend who kindly listened as I muddled my way through concepts and the initial plot framework. I am proud of this beginning. I believe there is great power in oral storytelling, and certainly we owe much to the ancient orators who told stories without benefit of keyboard or mobile devices. In my own life I still remember the feeling of peace I experienced when my mom would read aloud to a younger version of me and my brother, and the sound of laughter when my grandpa told a tale, and the wonder I felt while listening to the guest storyteller in my sixth-grade classroom—I couldn't believe she told an entire story without using a book.

The taggles were born out of my respect for the oral traditions. May this art form never be overlooked, or diminished. When the electricity goes out, and internet connections are lost, we will still possess the ability to dance and sing…and tell stories.

Thank you to the artists: Ben McSweeney first responded to my cover art inquiries; Chris McGrath introduced me to Eric Wilkerson who ultimately created an amazing book cover. Beyond his skills as an artist, Eric is genuine, professional, and gracious. Ron Wagner is a local artist who has literally painted half the town of Des Moines, and I am extremely pleased with the map he created for this world. These four men reinforce the general awesomeness of the art community.

Thank you to my editors: Floyd Largent, I was scared to death to put this story in your hands. You were the first to kick it around, and the last one to sign off. Thank you for the honest feedback, suggested changes, and genuine enthusiasm. Tracey Kelley, it's not easy to gut a novel, but you are exactly what I needed. Together we watched as several characters and entire sections hit the "cutting room floor." Thank you for the long discussions and creative energy. Nate Granzow, thank you for unicorns. You gave me hope that this story could appeal to a much larger audience, and your feedback was greatly appreciated.

Thank you to the various members of the Gateway Writing Group including: Jennifer Perrine, Craig Van Langen, Grant Cogar, and Patience Shattuck. And thank you Skip and Paul Asjes for your love of storytelling.

Lastly, thank you to my family, especially my wife, Jessica. You have read everything several times over and still you ask for more. You are my champion, and I am eternally grateful.

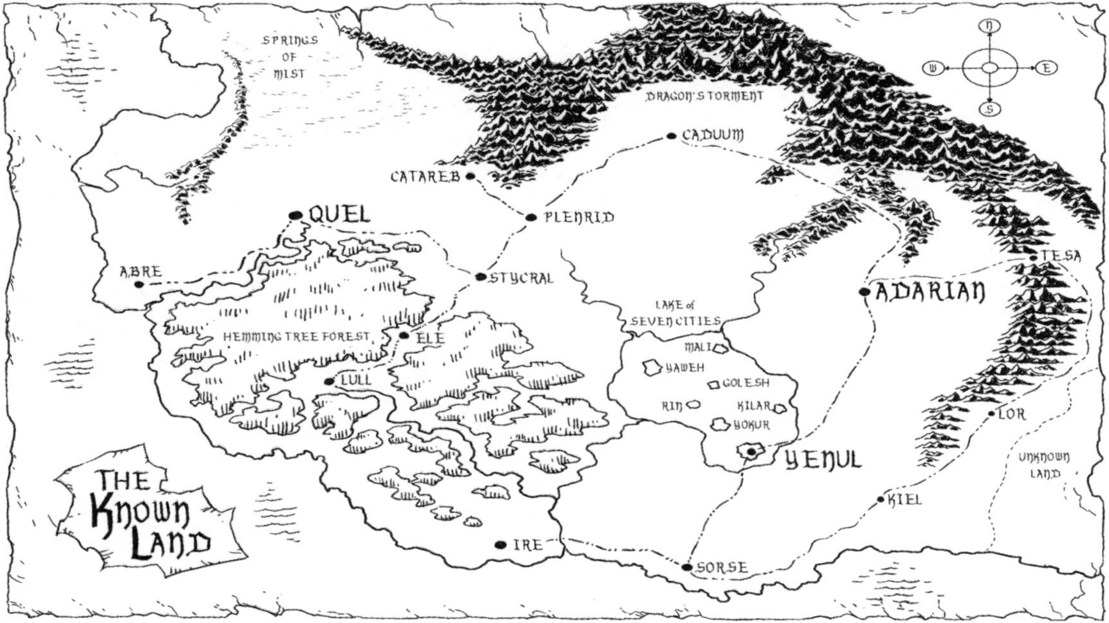

N
W
E
S
SPRINGS OF MIST
DRAGON'S TORMENT
CADUUM
CATAREB
QUEL
PLENRID
ABRE
STYCRAL
TESA
ADARIAN
LAKE of SEVEN CITIES
HEMMING TREE FOREST
ELE
MALI
YAWEH
GOLESH
LULL
RIN
KILAR
YOKUR
LOR
YENUL
UNKNOWN LAND
THE Known LAND
KIEL
IRE
SORSE

QUEL

a taggle's tale

As spoken by a taggle boy who stood in the streets of Lor, his shadow stretched toward Yenul when he began his tale and pointed toward Adarian as he finished. His voice was deep with uncommon maturity, pleasant to the ear. There was too much sadness in his green eyes, however, and his weakened posture was slightly distracting, but his crisp movements more than compensated. His name was Lucen. His brother died at Quel. He spoke in the manner of all taggles, for our story is a journey we share. May the Sphere forgive our mother and remember our father, as revealed in Dsal's vision.

- DK Vel

The barely-clad taggle boy repeatedly, if slowly, strikes the iron skillet with a wooden spoon, a source of audible irritation that morphs into emotional manipulation as the taggle reaches the climax of his tale, emphasizing it with a final *clunk*. It's a fine piece of storytelling. Before the boy began his tale the gathered warriors spun their discolored silver spoons around the edges of an unsatisfying breakfast consisting of large white globs of grits. The topis, all of them Adarians, started the morning wondering if this was to serve as their final meal before entering the seventeen-day-old battlefield surrounding the city of Quel. Whatever their thoughts, however, whether they dwelt upon images of lovers and young ones, cursed the Adow for leading them into war, or steadied their nerves with mental repetitions of sword movements, they were in no mood for a story. Yet, with the taggle's final strike of wood upon iron, as though it were a prearranged signal, every topi within earshot of the soiled taggle boy stands in solidarity. Discarding tin plates for drawn swords they raise their weapons to the smoke-covered sky and chant, "For Adarian! For Adarian!"

He is their ancient champion, the warrior for whom their city is named. The taggle's tale ends when Adarian dies in the arms of his Adow, giving his life to save her. That's how it always ends. That's why he is remembered. Before Adarian's death, those who served as First Etabli were *protector of the Adow* in name only, but Adarian died in battle. He died protecting his Adow. His act of honor generations ago, now recalled by the taggle's tale, is the reason the Adarian warriors stand and salute.

A trumpet beckons, silencing the chant. The Adarians quickly sheath their swords and march with organized haste toward the front lines where they will once again follow their much maligned Adow into battle. Regardless of her reputation, however, and even though the majority of the gossip originates from their homeland, the Adarians remain unquestionably loyal to their Adow; for while gossip is a recognized and time-treasured recreation among the Adarians, it does not advance one's political aspirations as quickly as an act of honor upon the battlefield.

The wan taggle boy, wearing only a black loincloth, is lost in the sudden flow of steel and leather. His story has inspired the Adarians, but he's quickly forgotten. Taggles are slaves, identified as such by their mutilated ears. As with all taggles, the boy's mother was placed under guard until she gave birth. Then a topi warrior carved into the boy's pointed ears, rounding them at the tip, forever marking him as a taggle. There are rumors that some have escaped the mark, some who live freely among the topis, but for most taggles their only sense of freedom is when they tell a story. They are the keepers of story, great orators allowed to share their tales with everyone but the Adow—never the Adow, for although a select few are chosen to serve the Adow directly they are forbidden to speak in her presence.

The taggle boy kneels down and reaches for the nearest plate, digging his fingers under clumps of poorly mixed grits, unappetizing to be sure, but he hasn't eaten since his master died five days ago. He shouldn't touch their food, it isn't allowed, but he devours three plates. Then he is pierced by the broad blade of an Adarian sword held firmly in the smallish hands of Birate, an aspiring topi warrior eager for advancement. But punishing a taggle's offense, his first kill, fails to elicit any reaction from the warriors who maneuver past him. There is no honor to be claimed. The crestfallen young warrior, who arrived at Quel two days ago, withdraws his sword and continues his unorthodox march, praying to the Sphere, pleading with his god for an opportunity to slay a rebel this day. Behind him, the taggle boy dies with his face in a glob of grits, vacantly staring at the tattooed markings on his knuckles that make up every taggle's prayer:

Remember our father
Forgive our mother

Thousands of Adarian warriors march past the taggle's body. Formed and reformed after five-years of war, the

161 Adarian divisions that remain, accounting for over half of the warriors in the Adowian Army, have suffered many losses. One division, the Adarian 6th, was completely wiped out three days ago. Nevertheless, their banner still hangs proudly over the entrance of two separate, now vacant, large green tents. The Adarian warriors, purposely marching past the tents on their way toward the smoke veiled city of Quel, kiss the back of their silver gauntlets in remembrance of their brothers.

The warriors form units as they reach the front lines of the greater Adowian force. Each division is led by a Rovet, a warrior who has proven themselves in battle. Still, the Rovets are not the *formal* leaders of each unit. That title belongs to the otherwise detested Madars, a blood-inheritance. The Madars, as is their custom, quietly hide in their luxuriously decorated maroon colored tents…far from the chaos of war.

Every Madar, that is, except Maldinado, Madar of the Adarian 45th.

Maldinado refuses to retreat.

"May the Sphere protect you," he says quietly to his life-long friend, Hintor.

"And keep you in His light," Hintor responds automatically. He is a farmer from Plenrid disguised as an Adarian warrior. His relationship with Maldinado allows him to serve in the Adarian 45th, usurping his lack of Adarian blood. He is thin, short in stature; his black hair the only physical trait he shares in common with the Adarians gathered around him…that, and their skill with a sword.

Maldinado, in contrast, is pure Adarian with his black hair and gray eyes, his sculpted jaw line. He is tall, thick in chest and shoulder. Serious. Focused. The Madar is slightly older than Hintor; even so they are yearlings, really, not yet warriors. And neither truly belongs in this battle.

"Why do we fight this battle, Maldinado?"

"For Adarian…and for Decrome." Maldinado points toward the Rovet of the Adarian 45th, a flat-nosed warrior with overly long arms standing a good distance in front of them. He is the leader of the Adarian 45th, not Maldinado. "And because I refuse to die in my tent as a coward like my father."

Decrome raises his sword and shouts, "The battle ends today!" The response is a roar that surges through the gathered warriors.

Then, in accordance with Adarian tradition, Hintor and Maldinado exchange swords with a promise to exchange them again at battle's end, a promise to survive. All around them, the stalwart warriors of the Adarian 45th make similar exchanges, though not everyone follows the tradition. One of the taller warriors, Halcromb, bare-chested under a grey beard that drips with the sweat of a two-day fever, refuses to exchange weapons with his son, Shamlon, a red-haired warrior standing beside him.

"No yearling, I'll keep my sword. I've no intention of surviving another day."

"Father!"

Halcromb pats his right thigh, blood-soaked bandages concealing an infected wound. "I'm already dead."

Shamlon nods his head with resignation, turning toward the front with new determination. "May the Sphere protect you."

"And keep you in His light."

Surrounding the highly respected Adarian 45th are the other Adarian divisions. Adarian 8th, generally considered brutes. Adarian 29th, known to capture and torture prisoners regardless of gender. Adarian 11th, strategists. Every remaining Adarian unit stands behind their Adow except the Adarian 41st which has long been an embarrassment to the city. Gan, Overseer of Adarian, hasn't allowed the 41st to leave the city since they mistakenly shot a barrage of arrows into the ranks of the Yakur 3rd at the Battle of Ire. Gathered around the Adarians are warriors from every city in the land including Lor, Abre, and Kiel. Only Quel, homeland of the rebel Yenen, a city twice as large as Adarian and known for its fine weavers and silversmiths, has chosen to stand in opposition to the Adowian Army.

Leading her forces, arriving to assume her place at the front, is the Adow. These are her warriors. This is her war…and the war ends today!

The Adow, along with Ayson, the newest and most polarizing First Etabli to ever assume the position, looks over the ranks of the Adowian Army. Their forces are much smaller than they were when she led them out of Yenul five years ago. *It can't be helped*, she convinces herself.

Both Adow and First Etabli are surrounded by the Adowian Guard, twenty warriors hand selected by the First Etabli to protect the Adow. Ayson wipes the sweat from his bald-head and secures his golden helmet. A scream rises from the battlefield, a dying warrior unseen behind a wall of smoke.

"Warriors shouldn't sound like that." Ayson says as his black horse shifts closer to the Adow.

"They're calling my name." The Adow slowly wraps her black hair around her finger, listening to the staggered moans of the dying. *My Adow! Save me, my Adow!*

Ayson takes her hand, pulling it away from her hair. She's shaking. "You don't have to do this."

"The walls have fallen, Ayson. We can't give Yenen another day."

God of Another World: The Adow

"I meant you don't have to lead the charge."

"You know that's not true."

The Adow raises his hand to her lips, kisses his clammy palm. "I'm fine. Yenen will be dead soon, and all of this will be over." She clings to his hand, unwilling to release it. Ayson hesitates before gently pulling his hand away to draw his sword. He motions for the march to begin.

The Adow's sword, the Sword of the Sphere, remains sheathed. No Adow has ever used the sword. One of the Adow—the one who reigned during the time when Fael was First Etabli, whose seal was a crowned warrior, is known to have practiced swordplay in her early years. But even that Adow never drew her sword in battle, and this Adow, whose seal is a crown between swords, has never been taught such maneuvers. She's not even wearing armor, choosing instead to march into battle wearing a traditional white linen blouse with golden doublet and matching trousers. After all, *I'm not here to fight.*

She's here to judge…or be judged.

She kicks her horse forward into a walk as Teyo, an Adowian Guard, blows a five-note tune on his trumpet, her pace quickens with the final high note. She longs to end this battle. She longs to know the judgment of her god, the Sphere. She needs to know she was right in choosing Ayson over Yenen as her First Etabli.

The Adarians lead the Adowian Army, following the Adow into the smoke, unaware of her misgivings and altogether unconcerned. They are Adarians! They fight for honor, not the Adow. Even Brink, the stout banner bearer of the Adarian 45th, who was given his position because he is the brother-in-law to Gan, Overseer of Adarian, marches proudly into battle. He too, like his Adow, has never drawn his sword—a fact disguised, if not completely concealed, by his duties as banner bearer. Nevertheless, he carries the banner of Adarian's most honored division, and because of this he garners respect from the entirety of the Adowian Army, though he is often the object of ridicule within the ranks of the Adarian 45th itself.

Not far from the banner bearer, Halcromb limps along on his infected leg. He refuses any assistance offered by his son, Shamlon, or any other warrior for that matter. His eyes are wide with an expectation of battle. Shamlon drifts slightly behind his father, capturing to memory the last details of Halcromb's life so he can describe them to his mother and sister. His father's altered gait…the mud splattered about his boots…his naked torso, his armor too badly damaged to wear any longer. Sweat runs down his back and arms, turned black by the smoke. *This* is his father.

In contrast, and some distance away, Birate marches within the ranks of the Adarian 45th as though he were a locust jumping from footprint to footprint. He searches for a glimpse of the city walls between the shoulders and arms of the warriors ahead of him. He has always been short for an Adarian, but what he lacks in stature he compensates with ambition. Today is the day he will finally earn the respect of the Adarians, the warriors around him who threaten to trample him down if he doesn't march at a better pace, regardless of the fact his father once served as their Rovet.

Maldinado and Hintor bring up the rear of the Adarian 45th, all but forgotten.

Ahead of them, the Adow tries to ignore the screams of dying warriors. *Save me, my Adow! Bless me, my Adow! Have mercy, my Adow!* She moves her horse over their swollen and mutilated bodies, refusing to look at them even as they grab for her. They plead with her. *Help! Please!* But what can she do? She reaches for Ayson's hand.

The First Etabli sees images in the smoke. Ghosts. Shadows. He strains his brown eyes, desperate to navigate a path. He motions for the Adowian Guard to fan out, fearful of an ambush. *It's Yenen's only option!* He lifts the Adow onto his own horse so that she is directly behind him, allowing her white mare to wander away and disappear. She wraps her arms around him, buries her forehead into his back, beads of sweat lubricating his golden armor.

A hulking figure emerges in the haze, a lone warrior suddenly revealing the enemy's position. Two Adowian Guards, Teyo and Yla, instantly converge upon the warrior. Ayson raises his sword to warn of an attack, but quickly lowers it as the warrior comes into focus. He is one of them, Tesha from the Rin 9th. He's wounded—badly burned, his eyes swollen to blindness, left to wander in pain and agonizing madness. The Guards fan out once more.

"What lies ahead?" Ayson asks, but Tesha is deaf. The ringing in his ears is the only thing he can hear, and he groans like a mule. He walks past the First Etabli into the ranks of the Adarian 45th. Decrome, realizing the severity of his wounds, mercifully buries his sword into the wounded warrior. Tesha's death is a gasp. A whispered *thank you*.

Decrome follows Tesha to the ground, kneeling beside him until he is dead. Then he pulls his sword from the body. It is an act of mercy from a Rovet known more for his courage than his compassion, but it proves to be his last, perhaps his only good deed.

A large stone, taken from the city walls and shot from a catapult, descends upon the Rovet of the Adarian 45th, crushing him with a force that leaves his body half-buried in the ground, only his elongated sword arm is visible.

Chad Michael Cox

Brink stumbles backward, but he maintains his grip upon the banner of the Adarian 45th. He stares at the remains of the Rovet, momentarily. Then he gathers himself anew. He turns the banner in a circle five times, alerting everyone, except Birate who is too short to see, that the Rovet has died.

"Decrome is dead." Maldinado points to the circulating banner.

"May the Sphere be with him." Hintor responds.

"And keep him in His light."

"Hey!" Hintor pats his friend on the back. "That leaves you in charge."

"No, another Rovet must be chosen. Adarians will never follow a Madar."

"Then today's your chance to become Rovet." Hintor insists.

Maldinado and Hintor march past Decrome, pausing long enough to register his death. He was selected as Rovet during the battle at Stycral after he beheaded the Rovet of the Stycral 12th. Decrome was proven, oldest among them. He outlived four Madars, and personally killed Maldinado's father while he slept in his tent.

For that, Maldinado is grateful.

The Adowian Army continues to march through the smoke, despite the debris being catapulted into the air, unseen before it tears into their ranks. Ayson navigates his horse through the smoke, the shield of the First Etabli, with its engraving of Erin's head, raised skyward to protect against the assault - a feeble defense against the threatening boulders.

Ayson can't see the Guards. "It feels like we're all alone."

The Adow kisses his back, her own sweat blending with the coolness of his armor on her lips. "I've never been

God of Another World: The Adow

alone."

Ayson turns his head, but he isn't looking at the Adow. He's searching. Where are the Guards? Where is the Adowian Army? He can't see anything in the smoke.

Far away from the Adow and her First Etabli, Hintor hears the wisps of arrows around him. He draws closer to Maldinado. The wall surrounding the city of Quel is upon them…surprisingly unscathed! The rumored breach isn't there! The assault grinds to a sudden halt. *And where are the Adow and her First Etabli!* Only the banner of the Adarian 45th is visible up ahead - always the banner bearer!

"How is it he never dies?" Hintor asks. "Brink's been carrying that banner all over the damn battlefield for three weeks—you'd think someone would use him for target practice."

"Right now we're the target." Maldinado looks upward. "We need to move."

"There's no breach!" An anonymous shout echoes through the Adarian ranks.

"Retreat, Adarians! There's no breach!" It's coming from above.

Maldinado doesn't retreat.

"Ignore the enemy," the Madar yells. "Find the breach!"

Hintor stares at him, surprised by his tone.

Maldinado shrugs his shoulders with feigned indifference. "Decrome is dead. Someone has to give orders."

The Adarian 45th responds by blundering through the smoke. They can't see their enemy above them. They can't see the arrows or the boiling pitch being sent down into their huddled ranks. Adarians die in the smoke and confusion, helpless. The assault becomes chaos as the rest of the Adowian Army eventually merges with the Adarians.

Maldinado's opportunity to seize control of his division

collides with the rising danger of completely losing his warriors in the panic. Strangers, topis from other divisions, gather around him. Warriors from every city crush together, shoulder-to-shoulder. They gather and huddle around the Madar. He can't walk! There are too many bodies!

"Find the breach!" Maldinado urges again.

"I'd love to, just as soon as I can move!" Hintor shouts.

Another volley of arrows streaks into their ranks. A soldier in front of Hintor is struck in the throat, dead. He isn't a warrior of the Adarian 45th. His name is…was Gilvan, an Adowian Guard with straw colored hair and a missing front tooth. Hintor watches Gilvan die, but the warrior's body, supported by Hintor and the rest of the Adowian Army pressing around him, remains upright.

"There it is, Hintor!" Maldinado declares with renewed vigor.

The breach is real! Maldinado can see it now through the thinning haze, but he can't breathe. The crowd is pressing tighter. Bodies everywhere! Hintor grabs at his arm but quickly loses his grip as the Madar is pushed away. The strain is too much!

"May the Sphere be with you!" Maldinado yells.

"Maldinado!"

The Madar is taken by the crowd, as Hintor finds himself being steered toward a wall well beyond the breach. The pushing is relentless. He can barely keep his feet under him…thrust into the wall with such force that it knocks the wind out of him. He tries to push, but the warriors of the Adowian Army are killing him. He can't breathe! Then a fresh brew of pitch is sent down, scattering everyone. Hintor gasps for air, his lungs filling with smoke.

"Tasa Ro!" he coughs.

Hintor searches for Maldinado, spotting him in the

breach. The suddenly heroic figure is face-to-face with his enemy, but neither is able to effectively use their sword in the crush. They're pushed passed one another without engagement.

"Well at least spit in his face, or something!" Hintor shouts, but the Madar is too far away to hear. And then he is gone behind the walls of Quel.

East of the breach, having strayed far from the battle, Ayson and the Adow exit the forest. They head toward the gold banner of Quel, a chance sighting through a clearing in the smoke, enabling them to regain their bearings. "The battle has begun." Ayson says.

The Adow can hear it, as well, a subdued sound of warriors clashing, a welcome replacement to the groans of the dying. She looks down at her pale skin. There is a faint glow emerging, a white light from within that she knows will shine brighter as they near the battle. It's the sign she's been waiting for! A sign that the Sphere approves of this bloodshed! For five years she's wondered, waiting for the sign. "Look, Ayson!" She holds her arm up so he can see. Her fears are gone. This will be the final battle. At last, the war is over. *Everything will be alright!* "Hurry!"

Maldinado, and the rest of the Adarian 45th, spill over the breech and into the city of Quel. The enemy greets them with desperate enthusiasm, but the attacking Adarians can sense an end to the battle. Maldinado pushes through a wave of silver-armored warriors, killing two before working his way into a cobblestone street. The houses here have been reduced to crumpled red stone with mostly burned thatch roofs. Maldinado looks around, assessing his surroundings. He's in a housing district west of the main gate. The city is badly damaged, and rows of dead bodies line the pitted streets. A yearling lies bleeding in the middle of a small garden, his hand still grasping a rope wrapped around a black spotted goat. To Maldinado's right, at the top of a slight incline, wagons, crates, and bags of grain form a makeshift barrier behind which a number of archers take aim. To his left, a torrent of warriors is running toward him, and more warriors run along the city walls. *You're late in shifting your defenses, Yenen!* Victory is at hand!

Maldinado runs toward the threat to his left, merging with the red-haired Shamlon who struggles to keep up with his grey-bearded father.

On the other side of the wall, Hintor rushes into the sea of warriors surrounding the city and is once again consumed by its flow. He navigates his way toward the breech like a fish swimming against the current, finally moving into the city. Then the battle is upon him. He uses his sword, or rather Maldinado's sword, as he was trained to do. He kills. He slaughters. He feels the weight of a body as it goes limp on his sword. The body slides off, lifeless. Another warrior attacks and Hintor kills. He searches for Maldinado, but the Madar is gone—taken by the flow of battle, or climbing the walls…or dead.

"Maldinado!"

Several minutes later, Birate finally enters the city. He stands atop a pile of crushed stone, searching for a fight, but the rebels are retreating. He runs after them, eager for the kill.

Outside the city, Ayson guides his horse along the red stone walls, holding his shield above his head to protect the Adow against any stray attacks. There is little chance of that, however. The Adowian Guard now maintains a much tighter perimeter around the Adow, more than a little panicked at having lost her in the first place. Aside from the Guard, however, there is the Adow herself. Her skin is glowing! How long has he wondered if he was really meant to be the First Etabli? But now the Sphere has spoken!

There is a pause in the fighting, an expectation. Perhaps curiosity. No one was certain how the Sphere would decide, until now. Would He bless the Adowian Army, or condemn it to death as He did at the Battle of Mali? At last, the Sphere has provided a sign. Ayson straightens his back, proudly presenting his Adow for all to see. *Yes, I am your First Etabli, and this is your Adow!*

No one is fighting.

Warriors on both sides follow the First Etabli and the Adow through the city of Quel. Others watch from their positions along the walls. Ayson keeps his horse moving through the housing district toward the city gates and into the market square. Here he weaves through rows of red tents serving as a makeshift rebel camp until he reaches a central golden tent—an obvious symbol of defiance. Only Yenen would dare adopt the royal colors.

"Here." The Adow says.

She releases her grip from around his waist, slowly ascending from the horse. She looks at all the faces who now worship her, finally rewarded for their faith in her. She continues to ascend until she is floating high above the rebel camp, a light for all to see, for all to know the Sphere approves of this war! And it ends today! She smiles, acknowledging her own doubts. When she chose Ayson as her First Etabli over Yenen she went against tradition, but she knew it was the right decision. She *knew* it was right! Now the Sphere is glowing within her body—proof that she acted with His blessing. She can feel Him, His warmth. She looks down at the golden tent, at her warriors scattered throughout the market square awaiting her judgment.

I was right!

"The Sphere is with you." She declares.

"And we are in His light!" The response is a collective chorus from the Adowian warriors.

The warriors from Quel listen with trepidation; some even drop their swords with the apprehension they are now fighting *against* the Sphere. Others strike anew, having long abandoned the Sphere to become Worshipers of Morlac, the god of another world.

The killing resumes. Ayson dismounts and moves into the battle like a wind brushing over fields of wheat, the enemy flees before him in fear, unwilling to challenge a champion anointed by their Adow, now confirmed by the Sphere.

Yenen watches from atop the city walls, his mouth slightly agape. A lack of emotion minimizes the general awkwardness of his facial features, but what he so ably disguises on the outside he is unable to control on the inside: hatred. He loved the Adow's mother! He brought comfort to her in her dying days! He was chosen by her to succeed Cidal as First Etabli! He was *chosen*! And this…this new Adow, this obstinate Adow has taken everything from him. Everything! And still the Sphere chooses to align Himself with her.

"So let it be known." He mutters.

He pulls a red-feathered arrow from his quiver, the color of Quel, the color of Morlac–his new god. He no longer follows the Sphere. He notches the arrow against the string of a heavy bow. Thick arms hold it at the ready, but the Adow is too far away! He lowers the weapon. He must get closer!

Maldinado, along with a group of warriors from the Adarian 45th, Brink still holding the banner high within their midst, pushes through a line of defense hastily assembled upon a set of stairs leading to the parapets above the city. The rebel warriors of Quel are powerful, though much shorter than the Adarians.

"If they had more discipline they would present a greater challenge!" Halcromb yells. Adrenaline fuels his assault, much to his son's astonishment.

My father's leading the charge! It's as though Halcromb's leg has been healed, he's not even limping! Shamlon fights proudly beside his father. *They'll make him Rovet after this!*

Maldinado, Brink, Halcromb, Shamlon, and most of the rest of the Adarian 45th advance upon the rebel warriors until, at last, they gain the parapet.

Yenen runs past them.

Warriors from both armies rally at the appearance of the rebel leader.

"Kill him!" Halcromb yells. "For Adar…"

The grey-bearded Adarian's rally cry ends in a gurgle of blood as a sunburned warrior pushes Halcromb off his sword, sending him over the edge of the wall. He falls away from his foe…away from his son…to his death below.

But Shamlon is unaware of his father's death. His own wounds have left him dying and slumped against the parapet. He searches for Halcromb amidst the closing darkness. *Forgive me father…*

Maldinado hacks away at rebel limb and sword.

In the city below, still chasing his friend, Hintor swings his sword and maims. He thrusts and kills. He's in the shadows of the wall, but he can't reach the stairs. He can't reach Maldinado! Quel and Adarian warriors fight on the ramparts above him, all around him. Bodies are everywhere, fighting, surviving, dying… Hintor searches for his friend, but all he can find is the banner of the Adarian 45th atop the parapet. Brink, at least, is still alive.

"Lucky bastard!" Hintor shouts.

Birate chases a warrior into an empty tavern. He was only about fifteen paces behind the rebel, but it gave him enough time to hide, forcing Birate to search for his first victim within the musty darkness: under wooden tables, stacked chairs, and eventually behind the cracked marble bar top imported at some point from Adarian. He swings his sword at every shadow, but there is no one there. A broken window signals the rebel's escape route, and Birate charges up the stairs, one at a time lest he stumble, to the rooms above.

Yenen stops running when he reaches the eastern wall that runs the length of the market square below. The Adow is less than fifty yards away! He raises his bow and aims an arrow at the creature he despises. She's floating above the fray. Still glowing! The light is blinding.

Maldinado escapes the horde and runs after Yenen. He watches the rebel leader take aim, and suddenly realizes his target is the Adow. *Tasa Ro!* The Madar raises his sword in a charging, mostly panicked attack.

Yenen releases the arrow.

Maldinado brings his sword crashing down, sending Yenen over the wall to the city below. But Yenen's arrow flies true, striking the unarmored Adow near the heart. Maldinado watches in horror as his Adow falls from the sky, her body limp. She crashes through the golden tent below, striking the ground with echoing force–the tent collapses around her.

The Battle at Quel is over.

The Adow is dead.

God of Another World: The Adow

YENUL

THE ADOW

The Battle at Quel changed everything. My mother is dead. Now I'm the Adow and my First Etabli, Ayson, my father…Ayson is moss, clinging to my every pore!

"Call off the Guard, Ayson!" And leave me alone.

A fierce rain coats my face as I walk toward a clearing in the forest, adding weight to my already long hair. I wish Troq was here. Troq was my guardian before I became the Adow, before Ayson, before everything. He called me Ovda, short for Daughter *of the* Adow. He was my caretaker. Each night he would hold me and tell me a story, his crinkled fingers warm upon my back, his quivering voice caressing my ears as I fell asleep.

I wipe the rain from my face.

Troq is gone. He isn't coming back! I woke up one morning to find him dead, and I was given to another guardian, Faunride. That's how it is–the Adow is protected by the First Etabli, and the Daughter of the Adow is protected by the next best warrior. When they die they're replaced. Troq just happened to live long enough to serve as my guardian. It could have been anyone. He was part of a tradition, nothing more. We all have our duties.

Tasa Ro!

So much has changed. Now I'm the Adow, the youngest to ever assume the role, and Ayson is my First Etabli. I barely knew my father two years ago, but after my mother died Ayson entered my room, slid into bed beside me, and assumed his role as my First Etabli…always beside me.

Moss.

Again I wipe the rain from my face. I prayed for sunshine, but apparently the Sphere doesn't bother with the weather, or maybe it's just me He doesn't bother with. Either way, I'm drenched. Aiya, my maidservant, made a valiant attempt to dress me in a more weather appropriate cloak, but I chose a simple blue vest instead. Dammit! I hate it when she's right.

Towering pine trees surround me, completely concealing the twenty guards, including Faunride, who scan the forest for any sign of danger. I suppose it's a comfort knowing he's…that they're there, but right now I just want to be left alone. Every second of the day I'm surrounded by warriors whose sole purpose is to keep me safe. An assassin killed my mother, so now they assume someone will kill me. For two years they've checked every room before I enter, tasted every meal. They scanned this same forest, yesterday, for an enemy who isn't even there! It's not like we don't make this trip every day!

"Call of the guard!" I yell again. But Ayson ignores my request same as he did yesterday…and the day before. I will never be alone, again. Thanks to Yenen.

I don't have any memories of my mother's assassin. When she appointed Ayson as her First Etabli, Yenen disappeared. My mother assumed it was the last she would see

God of Another World: The Adow

of him, but twelve years later the Overseer of Quel was murdered. Yenen had reappeared, seizing control of the city. He led his newly formed army from Quel to Stycral. Then he conquered Ele and Lull, effectively closing the northern trade route. My mother was caught completely by surprise. Two more cities, Plenrid and Catareb, fell before she finally mobilized her forces and began a march on Quel.

Five years of war.

Now my mother is a marble statue, sculpted by Beaug. It's all that remains of her. It stands as a giant that towers above me as I enter a large grass clearing almost completely covered with yellow and blue flowers. The flowers sag in the rain.

Fitting.

I've come to hate this place. I hate that it's become hallowed ground, a shrine to my mother. If anything, there should be a statue of Troq. This was our place! This is where he taught me to fly a kite, and later how to use a sword. Yes, he taught an *Adow* how to use a sword! It was our secret. The fact is I don't need a First Etabli. I don't need Faunride, or any of the rest of them. Hell, I'm a better swordsman than my father has ever been!

Still, my guardians surround me. They surround this clearing.

This is where I came when Troq died, before they could assign me another guardian. I didn't want another guardian. I wanted Troq. They searched for me for hours, the only time in my life I've ever been alone. It was Faunride who found me. It was Faunride who served as my guardian after Troq. But he stepped aside when my mother died, allowing my Father his rightful place as First Etabli.

Ayson stops halfway into the clearing, unwilling to come

any closer to the statue of his dead lover, a reminder of the Adow he failed to protect, causing the gap between us to widen. He may soon refuse to enter the clearing altogether, but for now I'll take what little personal space I can get, which isn't much so I hasten to widen the gap, eventually reaching the statue of the mother I despise.

Unfortunately, I look like her. We're remarkably similar in facial structure with soft cheeks that highlight our green eyes and fade into a rounded jaw line. Our nose is the width of a finger, and our lips are thinner still. Not just my mother. All of the Adow share a likeness to one another. It's how we're identified by the Sphere, confirmed as his chosen ruler. Our god. Our duty.

"Why don't you look upon your Adow, Ayson?"

"It's enough I come to this place." He turns his back to me.

No, actually, it's not enough. "One day it will be my face on this statue. Who will come to see *me*?"

"I won't do what you ask! I can't!"

Of course he can't. He doesn't *love* me like he loved my mother.

I look back to the statue. Her face. My face. I close my eyes and pray that when I have a daughter, *if* I have a daughter, she never has to experience such hell. It's not like I want to do it anymore than my father does, but we all have our duties. Yes Ayson, tradition over love.

Love died with my mother.

I open my eyes, ending my prayers with an unspoken curse. I don't know why I'm praying to a god who isn't there. I suppose it's because Troq taught me to pray, or because Faunride taught me to follow tradition.

An arrow slaps the rain.

It strikes me just below the collarbone. The stabbing

pain resonates into my throat. It's hard to breathe! I'm on my knees before my mother's statue, bowing before her like a damn taggle, struggling to find reality.

"Assassin!" Ayson yells.

I can't see my attacker, or the guards. The world is a blur. Another arrow lands to my right. They're trying to kill *me*? Why? I'm not her! I'm not the one who chose Ayson! I'm not my mother!

There is blood, my blood…dripping onto a yellow flower, crushed beneath my hand. I stagger away from the flower, willing myself to stand and confront my unseen enemy even as the guards rush into the clearing. Troq would want me to fight.

There is someone there…wearing a red robe. He's running toward me, fumbling to notch another arrow, but Faunride is there…the guards close in on him and he's dead before he can reach me. I clutch my arm. My wound.

Ayson is beside me, holding me, shielding me. My blood travels the length of the arrow shaft, drips with the rain…disappears into the earth below. *Why would they do this?* I need the healers. I need to leave this clearing. Walk! Dammit! I pull away from Ayson. Every step fills my stomach and lungs with pain, but I have to keep walking because there's no one to carry me to the healers. Not anymore. Troq is dead. Faunride wouldn't dare touch me. Ayson…doesn't care.

"Tasa Ro!" I can't feel my arm.

I exit the clearing, retracing my steps through the now circulating forest, scanning the wavering trees for would be assassins come to finish the kill, come to silence the oracle of the Sphere. If they only knew the truth–the Sphere doesn't talk to me. He never has…*I think I'm actually dying!* I can't breathe! Is this how it felt, mother? I stop walking.

Ayson runs up behind me.

"Take it out!" I yell.

"You'll bleed to death."

"Take it out!"

The arrow didn't penetrate completely. Ayson has to push it out my back. He might as well be driving it through my brain. The pain brings a blur of spots, and it's all I can manage not to pass out. He snaps the arrow tip off the shaft then pulls the blood-laden shaft back through the front. I grab a handful of my blue vest and press against the wound, resisting the impulse to pray.

Ayson tries to support me as I walk to the healers in Yenul, but I push him away. "It should have been you!" *Why are they trying to kill me?* "Why didn't you protect me?"

Because my father's never been good at that sort of thing.

Tradition.

THE ADOW

Leeches are the most disgusting aspect of a trip to the healers.

Scholars are the most annoying.

There isn't much difference between the two. After my mother died, almost immediately after I received the news, the Scholars came with their empty pages and black ink. They waited and listened. Breathing. Sucking my blood.

Initially, I told them the Sphere hadn't spoken. It was the truth, there was nothing to reveal, but they wouldn't leave. "Pray to the Sphere" they said. "Tell us what you hear."

"Nothing."

"Pray again."

It was obvious they weren't going to leave until I gave them what they wanted. I prayed again…nothing. The Sphere couldn't be bothered with my request. The Scholars watched me pray, judging my ability to communicate with their god. Was I truly the new Adow? Was I really the new Oracle? I had to give them something, so I told a story, one

Troq used to tell me about a tiger.

Thus, my first revelation became a retelling of the tiger and the hunter. It was easy enough. In Troq's story, the hunter disguised himself as a red cricket in order to kill the tiger, so I told the Scholars that the Sphere would one day appear, disguised in red, and He would destroy Morlac, the god of another world. They recorded the prophecy with eagerness.

The lies appeased them for a time. They left me alone, off to study their newly recorded revelation, but they came back. They always come back. Even here among the healers, ink dripping from their feathered quills, empty pages fully extended like a naked lover anticipating the first touch.

I struggle to sit up from the bed, reluctantly grabbing Ayson's hand to steady myself. He's standing beside the bed, guarding me–waiting for me to speak like everyone else in the room. Leech! The only story I can think of is the tiger and the five wolves. It doesn't matter. Any story, any drop of blood will suffice.

"When the Green Moon is complete, in Dragon's Torment you must seek. Five Arms of the Sphere will appear, five you will find." Names, they'll want names. "Madic Baltin, Pel F'rute, Sol Pedantic, Disen T'lade, and Adelic Hon."

Names from Troq's past: two brothers, his uncle, a cousin, and a nephew. I haven't thought about them for years. Now they'll forever be known as *Arms of the Sphere* because I designated them as such; because the Sphere refuses to speak, leaving me with nothing but lies.

The Scholars feast upon my words more than normal. Quick scratches suffocating the ruffling sound of their feathered quills. They stop and stare. Do they know? They don't say anything. They never do. Leeches don't speak, after all. The Scholars leave the room.

"You've given them a quest." Ayson says.

It's just a story, Ayson, not a quest. Troq would've understood. I lay down even as the healers appear with a bowl full of leeches. Tasa Ro! Leave me alone! Like a yearling, I pull the blankets over my head—no more leeches! Please.

"The Green Moon is complete." Ayson continues.

The healers pull at my blankets, but my grip is tight. Something inside me suggests this is irrational behavior for an Adow, that I should act differently, but I don't care. "No more leeches!"

The healers persist, tugging on the blankets, pulling them away from my outstretched hands. I immediately curl my head into my knees. "Kill them, Ayson!"

My First Etabli doesn't kill the healers. He's never killed anyone. He's good at *watching* people die, though, and apparently he's good at watching me bleed. He's as useless as a prayer to the Sphere!

"Ayson!"

The healers wrestle me into position, eventually managing to remove my bandages. One of the healers, his fingers like twigs, a wart on his thumb, reaches into the bowl of leeches and pulls out a brown blob of slime. The blob extends, dangling between the healer's thumb and finger. It's seeking blood. My blood.

"Faunride!" I know he is standing guard outside my room. He is always near.

The healer places the leech on my shoulder. I'd rather feel the arrow again.

I close my eyes and conjure up an image of Troq's face: white beard and bushy eyebrows. Brown eyes a shade lighter than his skin. The uneven wrinkles that fell away from his nose.

Chad Michael Cox

I open my eyes and look at Ayson. Bald. Beardless. Gutless. "What did you say?" I've regained control, my admittedly petulant fit temporarily suspended.

"Last night a new moon appeared. The Scholars are calling it the Spheric Moon."

"Why wasn't I told about this?" Why doesn't anyone ever tell me anything? Another leech touches my skin. I close my eyes. Troq's beard...

"You were sleeping, my Adow."

I open my eyes. The prophecy was just a story! A lie! The Green Moon has been around for 280 years, how was I supposed to know the moon was complete?

"We'll leave as soon as you are healthy." Ayson says.

"What?" It's all a lie!

The healers place another leech on my wound, a muted presence savoring my blood.

~

I've become my mother!

I'm leading my warriors into Dragon's Torment, leading them to their death because of a lie. They'll hate me just like they hated her!

No! My mother is a statue in the clearing ahead. I'm not my mother. It isn't my face on that statue. We look alike, but it isn't me they hate. This will be a good thing. A quest is always a good thing–it unites the land, gives the warriors something to believe in...

...until they realize the prophecy is a story...find out I can't actually *hear* the Sphere. He's supposed to speak to me, instead I'm telling stories about tigers that the Scholars have somehow turned into a quest! And someone is trying to kill me! Tasa Ro!

I stop to face my father, behind me as usual. "Why are you following me?" *Why are you even here?*

God of Another World: The Adow

"I don't understand, my Adow."

I shove him backward. Wow! Did that ever feel good! I shove him again with such force that he falls over, laying there in an awkward pile of legs and sword and armor. What did my mother ever see in him? *Love?* He's a useless old horse! The only leech I can't remove! I start pacing, daring him to get up.

"Why do you always follow me?" I yell. Then I start walking toward the clearing because I can feel tears coming. Not now!

I focus on the leeches. Leeches! Leeches!—their slick bodies on my exposed shoulder. My mother. My father. The Sphere. That does the trick. No more tears. And just in time. Ayson catches up to me and turns me around to face him. He's holding me, his fingers biting into my arm.

"Forgive me, my Adow."

I slap him and break free of his grip. "How many times have I come to this clearing? You always *follow* me. If it's your duty to protect me then *lead*! Enter the clearing before me! I wouldn't have been injured if you were doing your duty. Act like you actually *want* to protect me!" Are you listening Sphere? "Tasa Ro! We're heading to Dragon's Torment!"

This can't really be happening.

Ayson grabs my right arm, so I slap him with my other hand. Then he grabs that hand, too. I fight against his grip, but he pulls me closer to him, holds me.

"Forgive me, my Adow." I'm his daughter, not his Adow. His Adow is dead and she'll never forgive him!

I pull away and start heading toward the clearing, searching for assassins as I walk. Troq taught me enough. I don't need Ayson to protect me. Besides, I have Faunride. My faithful Faunride. And Teyo…the other guards. And the

Chad Michael Cox

Adarians. *The Adarians*! They love a good quest.

But this isn't a *real* quest. I stop walking.

What am I doing? I'm the last of the Adow. There's no Daughter of the Adow to take my place. We shouldn't even be going on this quest! Has anyone *ever* survived Dragon's Torment? Then again, will I survive if I stay here? Someone tried to kill me! Yes, the Adow has always been surrounded by the First Etabli and the Adowian Guard, but it was all for show. She was never in any real danger, but now–this! This is insane!

Ayson comes to a stop behind me. He motions to the guards who follow, and to the ones in the surrounding forest. Silently, they fan out in search of assassins. I watch them move through the trees, suddenly glad I'm not alone–more grateful than ever that Faunride is nearby. But they'll all die if we go to the Torment, every one of them. I can't ask them to do that.

I can't tell them the prophecy is a lie, either. I can't tell them I'm no better than she was…or worse. My mother never lied to them. She was a fool, but she never lied. They'll never recover if they find out I can't hear the Sphere. Not after Quel. I'll lose my guards, my army, all of them. Even Faunride. They'll all curse the Sphere and worship Morlac. Already, too many worship the god of another world. I can't let that happen. Troq would never forgive me. Neither would my future daughter. No! I need them to follow me, I need them to follow the Sphere, even if he doesn't exist, or they'll never follow her. I won't do that to my daughter. Not like my mother. There's no choice. They *have* to die for me. I'm the Adow.

My father moves to my side, scanning the forest. His protection is useless. He's an impotent warrior, unable to lead and incapable of inspiring others to follow. What I need is the Adarians...maybe promise them an Adowian Burial. Yes! To the warrior who finds the Five Arms of the Sphere. It won't matter that the Arms of the Sphere don't actually exist. The Adarians, and everyone else, will join the quest for that honor alone. It's perfect!

Faunride emerges from the trees walking with a familiar gait, his right foot turned slightly inward...his black skin all but disappearing behind his golden armor—always the most polished among my guardians. He's escorting an old topi with a face like a mole, poorly concealed by a yellow-stained beard. I can tell by his purple robes that he's a Scholar, come to record another prophecy. Great, more lies.

"Forgive me, First Etabli." Faunride says. "I found this Scholar in the forest surrounding the clearing. He says he must speak with the Adow."

That's right, Faunride, always address the First Etabli before the Adow unless she initiates the discussion. He's an absolute traditionalist, always has been, but it's annoying he never speaks to me directly. Annoying and somewhat comforting. Faunride is a constant reminder of how things used to be before Quel when he was my guardian—before the lies.

"I'm listening, Scholar."

Ayson and Faunride turn to me in surprise, but the Scholar speaks without hesitation. He stands proudly, with an arrogance I quickly decide I don't like. His knowledge has, obviously, inflated his ego. "Long ago, a prophecy was spoken..."

I knew I didn't like him. Scholars have a tendency to speak in a monotone language no one understands. He rambles on about the Green Moon and Dragon's Torment. There was a journey that he took. Failure. Death. I don't understand anything else he says for what feels like an hour.

"The Sphere has grown angry. Listen to my words! Your warriors…"

He is speaking, but I hear nothing…like the Sphere–except there's this white substance on his lips. It stretches and snaps as he widens his mouth. I feel the sudden urge to wipe it off.

"Some say there is a dragon caged within, that the winds are his breath and the rumblings are his attempt to break free of his chains, but I fear there is a creature in the Torment far worse than a dragon. When you find this creature you will die."

So I have that to look forward to. He doesn't realize the whole thing is a lie. He's studied my words and come to the conclusion that I'll die. Thanks. Knew that.

Faunride draws his sword and lops the Scholar's head off. My traditionalist: unwilling to let anyone condemn his Adow, and still my guardian. Our eyes meet for a moment, his dark eyes a depth of guarded emotion. He is concerned for me–the same look he had when he first found me after Troq died–when I wouldn't eat, couldn't sleep. He was worried. He told me Troq's death should be celebrated, not mourned. He didn't understand, still doesn't, but his insistence upon routine and tradition has its place. Back then he got me out of bed in the morning, forced me to face each day. Now he's the only thing that makes sense in this suddenly decapitated land. I watch the Scholar's body fall, the lump of purple robes. It serves him right–all of them. *Do they all want me dead?* Leeches! If it wasn't for the Scholars there wouldn't be a quest!

"Remove his robes and display his body in the market," I order. "Strike his name from the Chronicles of Yenul."

Faunride sheathes his sword.

Ayson, I can't help but notice, never even reached for his. Tradition.

Chad Michael Cox

a taggle's tale

As spoken by a taggle boy in front of the Bread and Stew tavern. His voice was a pitch too high, for he had yet to reach maturity, but the audience was gracious if also a little drunk. His movements were stiff, and his expression lacked enthusiasm, but the Sphere blessed him with a metal bucket upon which he drummed. His beat was deliberate, staggered for dramatic effect, and his timing was precise. His name was DK Vel, a younger version of this old taggle. I was in Yenul when the Adow issued her decree concerning the Arms of the Sphere. I spoke in the manner of all taggles, for our story is a journey we share. May the Sphere forgive our mother and remember our father, as revealed in Dsal's vision.

- DK Vel

"Adowian Decrees don't concern you," the warrior growls. "No one is going to read it for a taggle boy."

The boy wipes the spit from his face, still learning his lot in life. He runs off to find his father, and the warrior turns back to the task of posting the decree, leaves without glancing at the gathering crowd. One of the peasants approaches the posting and stares silently.

"What's it say?" someone in the crowd asks.

The peasant shakes his head.

"Find a herald!"

"There's one."

The herald approaches and motions for silence. The taggle boy sneaks back to within earshot.

Adowian Decree 1575

We seek the Five Arms of the Sphere. All who are able must journey to Dragon's Torment—to death or glory.

An Adowian Burial awaits the one who finds the Five.

An Adowian Burial! The taggle boy lingers on the thought. He is a descendant of Taggle, the First Etabli who betrayed the Adow, identified by the scars given to all taggles—their ears carved into and made round at the tip as they exit the womb. It's the mark of their bloodline, the curse given to them by the Adow because Taggle had an affair with Koyo, producing a male yearling. They're allowed to live because of their father, but their ears are a sign to all that their birth, their life, is not recognized by the Adow. They're not topis. They're taggles.

But an Adowian Burial! That would change everything…a funeral procession that travels the land, stopping at every city for a five day celebration before returning to Yenul where the body is burned in the Fire of the Sphere. It's an honor reserved only for the Adow, and for her First Etabli, and it was given to Beaug, sculptor of Adarian. But no one else has received such a burial. An Adowian Burial would change everything!

The taggle boy leaves the crowd…

~

…even as Hintor, disheveled and in a foul mood from lack of ale, returns to Yenul after visiting his father in Plenrid.

He leads his horse beside Lake Yenul, the *blood lake* as it's called. Erin's Fire, a flower with red petals and a white center, floats on the water. An overcast sky stretches downward in sheets of soft rain that evaporate before reaching the ground, as though not allowed to touch the surface of the lake. Hintor follows the blood lake south where it forms a river, continues along this path until it descends into the waterfall which conceals the entrance to Yenul.

The warrior of the Adarian 45th passes behind the waterfall, entering a tunnel that leads toward a giant cavern. Inside the cavern is a geyser that erupts into, and which forms the underbelly of Lake Yenul. The water is held above the cavern with an ancient magic cast and maintained by the Adow's sorcerers, allowing those below to see the fish, waterweed, and the red petals of Erin's Fire–providing the illusion of blood in the water. The geyser is a constant roar, drawing Hintor's attention while his horse navigates the cavern.

"It's a wonder we don't drown." He mutters.

There's a marketplace at the bottom of the geyser with roads that extend outward in twenty-three directions. Houses are hidden in those shadowed paths. And taverns! Three Horns Tavern–where Maldinado will be waiting for him. He'll have ale! The Madar, and newly appointed Rovet, is the only warrior of the Adarian 45th who stayed in Yenul, unwilling to take his two-month furlough. Then again, he's the reason the Adarian 45th is still in Yenul, unwilling to return home, unwilling to leave the newly appointed Adow.

Hintor pulls on the reins beside a posted decree, reads the Adowian Prophecy announcing the quest to Dragon's Torment. "She doesn't have enough enemies? She has to head to the Torment?" Hintor tears the post from the wooden pole. Spurs his horse toward the mineral caves. "She's as obstinate as her mother!"

God of Another World: The Adow

Behind Hintor, far enough to remain unseen, a taggle boy follows. The boy maintains his distance, and he's careful not to look any topis in the eye. It doesn't matter. No one notices him. He's thin, and his neck sinks into his collarbone, exaggerating and elevating his shoulders. His nose extends from his face like the handle on a pot, making his eyes look all the more concave and beaten. His hair is black and sawed off to keep it short. He wears a black breechcloth, but the rest of him is bare. On his hands, covering each knuckle, are the symbols that make up the taggle's prayer:

Remember our father
Forgive our mother

The boy freezes as Hintor stops to buy two pairs of emerald earrings and some bread. The taggle studies the warrior's features: eyes folded under a drooping brow, a scar that crosses his nose and down his right cheek, black hair pulled tight and braided. A series of tiny scars along his right jawbone that interrupt the growth pattern of a fresh beard. He's wearing a green tunic and matching cloak.

Hintor places the earrings into his saddlebags. If they're heading to Dragon's Torment that means they will journey first to Adarian. Kaletine and Belur would never forgive him if he didn't return to Adarian with gifts in-hand. He bites into the sourdough bread. It isn't ale, but it's heavily salted and the crystals move across his tongue, reviving the saliva glands in his mouth. He swallows and feels the bread move slowly down his throat into his empty stomach. He hasn't eaten for two days, having exhausted his food supply because he gave it to a beggar along the road to Yenul.

"Probably a thief." Hintor had muttered as he rode away from the beggar, cursing his act of kindness with the knowledge he would go hungry until he reached Yenul.

Chad Michael Cox

A two-day fast was better than the guilt he would have felt over letting a fellow topi starve to death, however. The guilt was a gift from his father, the result of a *proper* upbringing.

Hintor enters the mineral caves of Yenul, the crowds thinning significantly as he moves through the silver-speckled tunnel. Even so, the warrior doesn't notice the taggle boy who follows him. The walls of the cavern, rich with unmined silver by order of the Adow, provide a subdued glow that increases as he approaches the well-constructed Three Horns Tavern. It's the only structure in Yenul that was erected using timber, making it a favorite of the Adarians who, generally speaking, prefer to spend their lives above ground. Hintor, being a farmer from Plenrid, has never understood how anyone could live here. Everything in Yenul is carved out of the rock, even the Adow's palace, to hear the Adarians tell it, is a series of caverns and tunnels. Hintor dismounts, leaping from the horse, and hands the reins to the nearest taggle boy, the one who followed him. Then he heads inside the tavern, its main decoration a full-sized bronze sculpture of a three horned ram. He finds Maldinado sitting at a wooden table along the back wall.

He has ale.

"She wants to die!" Hintor greets him with the decree and reaches for the nearest mug.

Maldinado nods. "I've seen it."

Hintor takes two gulps of ale, not enough to improve his mood. "It'll be worse than Quel. I won't go!"

Maldinado stands to hug his friend. "How was your trip?"

Hintor drains the rest of the mug and slams it onto the table. "You've already enlisted us, haven't you?"

God of Another World: The Adow

"I had to, I'm an Adarian." Maldinado grabs two more ales from a passing server, handing one to his friend.

Hintor grabs both. "I'm not."

"That sphere burned into your chest says you are." Maldinado reminds him of the mark he received when he joined the ranks of the Adarian 45th, matching the one on his own chest.

"Furmec Ro!" Hintor drinks more ale. Both mugs. All of it.

Maldinado sits down, and motions for Hintor to join him. "How's your father?"

"Mardtbren sends his blessing." Hintor grabs a passing mug, but he doesn't drink it immediately. "Something tells me we're going to need it."

"It's good to have you back." Maldinado says. "I've been drinking alone for too long."

Hintor stares at his friend. Maldinado's beard looks as though every hair is being pulled from his face. The yearling he knew is gone. "It wasn't your fault her mother died, you know. It was the will of the Sphere. And you sure as hell won't be able to protect this one while you're busy trying to survive in Dragon's Torment!"

Once again, Maldinado sees Yenen release the arrow— reliving the moment forever frozen in his memory. They anointed him Rovet because he killed the rebel leader. But it was Yenen's arrow that killed the Adow. Maldinado was too late. Never again!

"What do you know about the will of the Sphere?" Maldinado chides. "You've never prayed a day in your life."

Hintor shakes his head. "That's not true. I pray for your sister and those yearlings everyday." He finishes the ale and signals a taggle girl to bring them more, though his enthusiasm is wavering. He can feel his stomach sloshing around as though it were a water skin hanging from the saddle. "They've lived a hard life."

Maldinado lowers his empty mug, waits for Hintor to continue, but his friend stares off into the crowded tavern. The scars on his face have greatly disfigured the farmer he once knew, the yearling who fell in love with his sister, Nataline. Maldinado turns to the window beside the table, its blackness reflecting his own face. He stares at his grey eyes, the warrior he's become–the warrior his father never was–Rovet and Madar of the Adarian 45th!

"I have to go on this quest." Maldinado says.

"I know." Hintor's mood is finally subdued, his attention momentarily distracted at the sight of Birate picking a fight with a much larger stranger. "And I'll be right beside you like a fool." He takes another sip even as Birate takes a swing. "Please tell me we don't have to take little Birty with us." The stranger sends Birate skidding across the floor, unconscious from the looks of it.

Maldinado turns at the commotion. "You've got to admire his determination."

"Like watching a toad attack a dragon." Hintor raises his mug in toast to the stranger, grabbing his attention. "I'll drink to that!"

Outside the tavern, the taggle boy who followed Hintor spots a group of six taggles mingling around the back door. The boy joins them and introduces himself as DK Vel, thus beginning his quest for an Adowian Burial.

God of Another World: The Adow

a taggle's tale

As spoken by the oldest living taggle in the Abre dallic. He was 72-years old. A thin white beard reached down to cover his swollen stomach. He spoke slowly and with great patience, allowing the audience to absorb both the rhythm of his voice and the meaning of his words. During his tale, a fly landed upon his beard, another on his shoulder, but his voice was so alluring that both flies sat as though in a trance. It was a perfect telling. His name was Treth. His sister once served the Adow, but she could not have known all the details in this story, for only the Adow knows the words spoken between herself and the First Etabli in moments of solitude. But his telling is consistent with the stories we know for certain, thus I have preserved his tale. The old taggle spoke in the manner of all taggles, for our story is a journey we share. May the Sphere forgive our mother and remember our father, as revealed in Dsal's vision.

- DK Vel

Ayson wipes his brow, interrupting the images of Quel that flood his thoughts. The day is warm and the tunic under his armor is already damp. The Adowian Army heads to Adarian, where thousands more will join the quest. Quel changed many things, but some things will seemingly never change: Adarian honor and Adarian pride.

Adarians love to fight, but they love a quest even more than a battle. There is more honor in a quest, after all. At least there is more honor to the one who completes the quest, and the one who completes this quest will be as honored as their beloved First Etabli, Adarian, hero of Ire.

First Etabli. Ayson mouths the name. A title. A great honor. Throughout history the First Etabli have protected their Adow. Erin, the First Etabli. Anine. Aul. Taggle, the cursed. Ylaf. Erbohn. Ig-poy. Adarian, hero of Ire. Fael. Irloore. Cintyge. Lio. Enyure. Athoyen. Ferya. Cidal. Ayson, of Quel.

Ayson is the only one to witness the Adow's death. Even Taggle, even *he* died in the arms of his Adow. *Ayson* lives. *Ayson* is riding at the front of the Adowian Army. *Ayson* departed Yenul with the army two days ago. *Ayson* is their champion.

Under the sun, the golden armor of the army is a sea of shimmering brilliance, a glow meant to bring glory to the Sphere. The colorful banners of each division are held high, but there is no wind to unfurl their colors. There was a time when they were not so limp, a time when they rode with purpose, when they followed their First Etabli with vigor. That was before Quel.

Ayson looks at the Adowian Guard. Faunride, Teyo, Valin, and Yla surround the Adow. The others patrol the perimeter. They are all strong warriors, stronger than their First Etabli. He looks down at the shield secured just behind his left leg—an image of Erin, the First Etabli. He looks back at the Army. They don't follow him. They have never followed him. He is Ayson, of Quel. He is not Adarian, hero of Ire. He is not Cidal. He is not even Taggle, the cursed.

Ayson glances at his daughter. She deserves the joy of

a wedding day. She longs to design her Leet Socno. He is the one who denies her this joy. Ayson remembers his own wedding day. The banner-like Leet Socno was placed over their joined hands and then hung above their doorway… until she died.

Faunride kicks his horse, moving into the tree line. Ayson knows he will relieve the scouts. Faunride is a good warrior. A fine guardian of the Adow.

Ayson motions to the remaining guards. They fan out in a circle until they are out of earshot. "You deserve better, my Adow. You deserve a wedding, and a Leet Socno, and a daughter. I wish I could provide all those things for you."

"You can provide me with a daughter." The Adow says. "According to the Scholars you're the only one who can do that."

"I can't." Ayson looks down at his hands. They are clean, without callous. "I can't." He says, again. He isn't her First Etabli. Not *hers*. It wasn't supposed to be this way. Surely, the Sphere never intended it to be this way.

"Then why bring it up?"

"I wish things were better. You deserve more."

"I deserve what I've received, Ayson. It's what the Sphere chose for me. There's nothing more to discuss."

First Etabli. Champion of the Adow. He is the only one permitted to touch the Adow. To love her. To give her a daughter, as declared by the Sphere. "Forgive me, my Adow." It's a whisper she cannot hear.

They ride in silence for the remainder of the day.

After dinner, Faunride enters the Adow's tent to give a final report for the evening, careful to avoid looking at the Adow who is undressing in preparation for her bath. He tells Ayson that the army has completed camp preparations. Two warriors and their horses were killed when a cylen tree fell unexpectedly. No deserters have been reported. The Stycral 14th has arrived, and they have joined what remains of the Golesh 47th. Eshion has been promoted to Rovet. Finally, "the sorcerers have requested that they be moved to the south of camp. They feel the land they currently occupy is too rocky."

"This is turning into a nightly ritual," Ayson grumbles.

"Isn't that the case with sorcerers, First Etabli? At least in my experience."

"All right, let them move. Who's over there now?"

Faunride glances down at a scrap of parchment paper. "The Golesh 13th has stated their willingness to accommodate this request."

The Adow slides into a silver tub. "Give them my blessing." She says. Faunride starts to acknowledge the Adow then quickly turns away. "At once, my Adow."

Ayson grins. "And it wouldn't hurt my feelings if someone forgot to wake the sorcerers in the morning…at least until the rest of the Army has moved on."

Faunride gives an auspicious nod. "I'll invite their leader, Galinor, to a game of 5-Ruby, tonight. I'll make sure he drinks plenty of ale."

"How is the game progressing?"

"The Yowt Ruby is naked, and there are four peach pits aligned to the Rhil Ruby."

"Place a wager for me. The Unern Pattern will be rolled tonight." Ayson hands Faunride a pouch of gold coins.

"Of course, First Etabli, but the boar tusks haven't rolled in my favor for two nights. Perhaps you would rather place the wager yourself?"

"No, it is better that you do it. May the Sphere bless you."

"And keep you in His light." Faunride bows and exits

the tent, leaving Ayson to his nightly prayers. He kneels beneath a makeshift altar suspended from the top of the tent consisting of a golden candle set within a glass aureole. His prayers become thoughts that drift as easily as the smoke from the candle. When was the last time the Adow knelt beneath the altar? Why didn't those two warriors move out of the way of the tree? How does that even happen?

Behind him, the Adow's maidservant, Aiya, bathes the Adow. "Tomorrow I think we put some hot oils in your hair. It will keep it healthy. You travel in the open too much. It's not good, so much dust from the horses and wagons."

"Feel how dry my skin is," the Adow says.

"Mine too."

"My arms are so dry they itch. I was scratching them all day."

"I give you a cream. I stole it from my sister before we leave. I used some this afternoon and I already feel better."

"Aiya, you're such a blessing. I always miss you when you leave. Where did your sister find it?"

"It was selling in the market in Broken Tunnel. She got plenty so she don't mind me taking it."

"How is she doing? Were the healers able to help her breathing?"

"She has good days and bad. I don't think they help much, but they give her remedies."

"Don't even talk about remedies! Leeches! I'm going to outlaw the use of those things. Disgusting having them crawl all over you, sucking your blood. I can't even think about it!"

"You'll never get leeches on me. I die before they do that. And I wouldn't let them use leeches on my sister, either."

Ayson rises from beneath the altar, tired of the conversation...hair oils and creams? Leeches? He walks over to the gefor and relieves himself, then moves to the entrance of the tent. He opens the flap.

"First Etabli!" The Adowian Guards rise from their game of 5-Ruby and bow in unison, awaiting orders.

He looks beyond them at the tents...the row of torches and the night sky, the distant shadows of the land touching the stars. There was a time when he wondered what was beyond the horizon. Now he knows.

Faunride moves forward. "First Etabli?"

Ayson stirs from his thoughts. "I placed a wager on the game. I thought I'd watch for a while and see if the Sphere has blessed me tonight."

Faunride bows dutifully. "The First Etabli is eternally blessed."

Ayson nods his head in response, signaling the guardians to return to their game. He watches them play, huddled close enough together to cause a consistent, almost harmonious, clink of armor. Their movements are simple: a throw of the boar tusks, a drink of ale. Their laughter is hearty, one more so than the others. Ayson and Faunride exchange a grin at the sight of the black-robed Galinor, leader of the sorcerers. He is full of mirth, beads of ale falling from his long white beard. He will sleep well, tonight–oversleep, in fact. He'll be late in arousing the other sorcerers in the morning, and they'll likely struggle to catch up with the rest of the army. With any luck, they'll return home. Sorcerers are good for amusing tricks like the blood lake in Yenul, but they're useless in a fight and entirely too demanding for Ayson's liking.

His attention returns to the game which proves entertaining enough, but he remembers more stories being shared among the participants in the days when he used to play every night...before he became First Etabli. He shouldn't have joined them. His presence is making them uncomfortable. He's no longer one of them. Even so, he makes a few more wagers, guessing at the pattern of the boar tusks.

Faunride deposits the three tusks, miniature marble carvings resembling boar tusks, into a wooden cup before throwing them into a small circle made of string. Two of the three land inside the circle. Teyo, serving as overseer of the contest, confirms the Rhil pattern has been thrown. Damn! Ayson guessed all of them would land inside the circle in the Unern pattern, trusting in Faunride's practiced throwing technique. Nevertheless, he laughs at the chatter that rises from those who guessed right. He is glad for the respite, and the ale.

Teyo hands him the wooden cup. "It's your turn, First Etabli."

Ayson fills his mug with more ale before taking the tusks and turning toward Faunride. "It's been a long time since I've thrown the tusks, Faunride. You may want to change your wager."

"I've already changed to the Begn pattern." Faunride hands Teyo a silver piece, completing the transaction. "I just need you to land one of the tusks, First Etabli."

Aiya emerges from the tent, works her way through the crowd of warriors, and brushes past Ayson without a word. She is crying, or rather trying not to cry. She steps right into and through the circle kicking away half the game pieces. Then she is gone, off to her own tent. Ayson has never understood the handmaiden.

There is a scramble to retrieve the game pieces, including three rubies and five peach pits. Finally, Ayson throws the tusks. As predicted, all three land outside the circle.

Teyo confirms the result. "No pattern has been thrown."

"I fear the Sphere is not with me, tonight. Thanks for the ale, Faunride." Ayson says.

The Guards rise and bow, "First Etabli."

Ayson enters the tent. First Etabli. Again he lingers on the title. He stands in the shadows, listening to the warriors. Listening for comments about him. Innuendos. Ayson wipes his forehead and waits.

The Adow is resting on a bed of animal skins. She is lying on her side, facing away from him like she always does, but tonight she's wearing a red silk gown that exposes her back. Her black hair, normally pinned into a bun for sleeping, is spread wide. Candlelight flickers over her body. She's the very image of her mother, but it's not enough to forget she is still his daughter.

Ayson removes his sword and climbs into the circular bed beside her. They fall asleep facing opposite directions—the royal pattern. A taggle girl stands off to the side, fanning them with large green leaves.

THE ADOW

Ayson leaves the tent like a weed thrown from the garden. I start laughing, causing Aiya to pause in her scrubbing of my back.

"Have you grown ticklish?"

I shake my head. "No, Aiya." I look at my handmaiden with new perspective. Her black hair held tight in a bun above her head. Her green eyes. That perfect skin—mine is always so dry. Those adorable ears. "I've just realized how much of a blessing you are." She looks like my mother. She looks like me! Ayson can't stand her.

Aiya starts scrubbing my back, again. "I'm only your servant, my Adow."

"You're more than that!" I pretend to be offended. "You've been with me since I became the Adow." But what does a handmaiden truly know? She doesn't know me like Troq did. I've never told her anything important—that I can't hear the Sphere...that I question if He even exists. I place my hand on hers. "You're my closest friend."

"I'm glad to be your friend." Aiya drops the brush in

favor of a bucket which she dumps over my head.

I watch the water drip from my hair, my eyebrows. She's my only friend. A handmaiden. Not much to brag about. She *has* to be friendly.

"What do you think about this quest?" I ask. Aiya has never actually given me her opinion, in many ways she's not much better than a taggle, but she allows me to work out my thoughts and I have to admit I've missed her. She's been tending to her sister for too long.

"What do *you* think about it?" Aiya pulls her white sleeves down and takes a towel from a taggle girl.

Lies. They're lies, Aiya. That's what I want to tell her.

I stand to exit the tub, my thoughts drifting to the pink scar below my shoulder. I press my finger against it. There's a void underneath, a piece of me the leeches sucked out. Is this what the Sphere wants? Am I to be the last Adow?

"I think a lot of warriors will die." I finally respond.

Aiya wraps me, helps me out of the tub, and lifts my chin. "It don't matter, I think. Those warriors are willing to die for you. More than your mother could say, and anything that brings this land together is something worth doing."

"Even if it means going to Dragon's Torment?"

"Ask me again when we get there." Aiya smiles and pulls a sleeping gown over my head. It's red. I suppose I'm indifferent to the color, but Aiya always chooses red if it's available.

"Why do you like red so much?"

Aiya turns me around, guides me to a chair, and starts combing through my hair. It's tangled, but she has a gentle stroke. "I don't like red, but you look so beautiful in it. I could never wear red the way you wear it."

"But you do wear my gowns, Aiya. They always smell like you."

God of Another World: The Adow

THE ADOW

She stops brushing.

I turn to measure the impact of my words. That's right, Aiya. *I know your secret.* Could you have been so naïve? She struggles to look me in the eye, a moment of fear.

"It doesn't bother me. In fact, it makes things easier. When we get to Adarian I want you to go into the marketplace. Try on everything, and purchase anything that fits."

She struggles to smile. I turn back around and she resumes brushing.

"Thank you, Aiya. You can go now."

She bows like a dutiful servant. A moment later she is gone, and I'm all alone.

I know her secret…does anyone know mine?

I stand and walk to a gold-framed mirror leaning against a large wooden chest. The face of every Adow is reflected in my own. We are the Oracle of the Sphere, servants to a God who doesn't speak. Seventeen Adow came before me. At times I can see all of them, each face a slight alteration, layers of reflection composing my own. We are nameless, identified only in relation with our First Etabli. *She who reigned when Enyure was First Etabli.* Or by our chosen Adowian Seal, variations of crown and symbol: *Crowned Rooster* or *Crown over Sphere*. Unperceiveable differences! We have no identity apart from each other. I have their face. I speak with their voice. I wear the same clothes they wore…so why don't I hear their god?

Chad Michael Cox

a taggle's tale

As spoken by a taggle woman on the Mali coastline. It was windy, causing the Lake of Seven Cities to swell with great waves, but the woman's voice was hearty enough to rise above the distraction. She didn't stand, for she was with child, causing some in the audience to miss several key expressions. All the same, her wide brown eyes sparkled and burned - indeed they conveyed vibrant emotions; and the violence of the sea was a truly inspired backdrop for her tale. Her name was Jin. Her father served the Adarian 45th. She spoke in the manner of all taggles, for our story is a journey we share. May the Sphere forgive our mother and remember our father, as revealed in Dsal's vision.

— DK Vel

The sun is setting, and the sky is blazing pink with streaks of red. Hintor sits on a hill, facing north, watching the blood grass move in waves just beyond the camp of the Adarian 45th. His tunic is untucked, and there are visible patches of sweat on his back and chest. He is drinking warm tea from a leather cup, wishing it were ale with every sip.

"I used to run through these fields as a yearling." Maldinado joins Hintor and hands him a bowl of gray gook. He sits down beside his friend, skimming a spoon over the stew. "They say each blade represents a drop of blood for every Adarian warrior who has died in battle."

"Is that how you want to be remembered? As a blade of grass some yearling tramples?"

"I would die a thousand deaths if it meant the Adow was safe."

"She won't survive Dragon's Torment, you know. And neither will we."

Maldinado smiles. "We survived Quel, didn't we?"

Hintor tastes the stew. It's salty, lots of beans but no meat. "I survived. You've never been the same."

"I guess I see things differently, now." Maldinado raises his bowl. "Like food. My mother used to go days without eating. She said her hunger fueled her prayers to the Sphere. I never understood what she meant before Quel. Now I understand. I've been praying ever since Quel. I've been faithful to the Sphere. Five prayers a day. Every cleansing. Every fast. So the next time I have the chance to save the Adow, the Sphere will bless me."

"Oh, wise one." Hintor grins. "Where would I be without you?"

"You'd be a blade of grass in that field. No doubt covered in horse muck!"

"That field is for true Adarians." Hintor points out. "I still have Plenrid blood in me, remember?"

"I forgot about that. You haven't reminded me for at least a week."

"It's all that praying you do. I can't get a word in."

"If you were a little more faithful, I wouldn't have to

pray so much."

"That's what I like about you. You've always been able to overcome my faults. Besides, it doesn't matter how faithful I am. The way I figure it, with you and Nataline praying for me, the Sphere has to bless me"

Maldinado raises his bowl, once more. "He already has. You have food to eat, don't you?"

"Is that what we're calling this? You know, the other Madars are enjoying their own personal feasts, right now. We could be eating a roast with gravy, or warm biscuits—I like warm biscuits."

"Are you asking me to act like other Madars?"

"I'm merely pointing out the fact we could be drinking ale instead of tea."

"We?" Maldinado asks. "Madars don't share their meals with farmhands."

Hintor shrugs and takes a bite, uncertain as to what it is he's actually chewing. "Have you heard from Nataline?"

Maldinado nods. "I received a note this morning. She's made tunics and gloves for both of us, and she'll meet us at the greeting rituals."

"Is she bringing the yearlings?" Hintor asks.

"She didn't say, but we'll be in Adarian for a month, so I'm sure we'll see them."

Hintor scrapes his bowl and takes the last bite. "I hope she brings bread."

"Have you ever known her to *not* bring bread?"

"I should have married her when I had the chance."

"You never had the chance."

"Where did she learn to cook? Not from Breline. I can't remember your mother ever cooking a meal."

"I'm not sure. She was born with the ability, I guess. She made her first pie when we were yearlings. I've never tasted a better one." Maldinado cocks an eyebrow. "Though I've never tasted a pie made by the Adow."

"She doesn't cook. She has servants to handle that."

"True, but if she *did* cook, I bet it would taste better than my sister's finest bread."

"I don't think that's possible." Hintor stands. "They're starting a new 5-Ruby game, tonight. You coming?"

"Not tonight. I need to pray."

"You're turning into your mother."

"Better her than my father." Maldinado stands and hands his empty bowl to a taggle boy standing nearby.

"Don't ever become your father." Hintor gives his bowl to the boy then turns to leave. "Do you want me to place a wager for you?"

"Place it on the Rhil to be the first naked ruby."

"Sure? Brink's aligned to the Rhil ruby. You know how lucky he is."

"I'm sure."

"Alright, it's your gold." Hintor departs with a shake of his head.

Maldinado retrieves his rucksack from the ground beside him and heads down the hill just as Birate is coming up. The little warrior is walking hand in hand with a Scarlett, one of a hundred or so who have made the journey from Yenul. More will join the caravan at Adarian, fully aware that the warriors receive weekly payments for their services and, more importantly, there are only two options for spending that gold within an army camp: gambling and female companionship.

Birate stops in his tracks upon seeing Maldinado, his efforts to sneak back to his tent suddenly thwarted. He releases the hand of the Scarlett, a disheveled blond wearing a leather vest over her otherwise naked torso. "My

Rovet, I found this Scarlett wandering the perimeter. I was escorting her back to the camp."

Maldinado wonders what it must be like to have a father he so desperately wanted to emulate, rather than living with his own father's sordid legacy. Birate's father was Rovet of the Adarian 45th before Decrome. He was so well respected, in fact, that Gan, Overseer of Adarain, personally attended Birate's First Cleansing as a favor to the Rovet. The Adarians spent months spreading that particular piece of gossip to the point that most believed the Rovet had betrothed his son to the Overseer. But whether or not that is true, Birate never fully grew into a man's body, though apparently tonight he is hoping to become one.

Maldinado stifles a grin. What would Hintor do in this situation?

"You must have been on your way to relieve Gan-Pi from guard duty, then." Maldinado adopts an official tone. Birate, standing there with his scraggly brown beard poorly disguising his youthful features, is relieved to find that his lie worked. "Very well, I'll escort the Scarlett and leave you to your task."

"He did nothin' of the sort!" The Scarlett turns on Birate. "This yearling wanted to keep things quiet like. Didn't want no one seein' me."

"I trust you charged him extra, then?" Maldinado asks.

"I don't know what she's talking about." Birate stammers.

The Scarlett pulls a bag of gold from her belt and smiles at Maldinado. "Charged him three times the normal rate. Didn't like him bein' embarrassed about the whole thin', ain't right to be sneakin' around."

"Not everyone is, shall we say, experienced in such matters." Maldinado manages not to laugh. "I trust this doesn't

God of Another World: The Adow

sour the reputation of the Adarian 45th on the whole?"

She slides the coin pouch under her belt, once more. "Of course not."

"Good!" Maldinado turns to Birate. "You'll find a barrel of Stycral wine inside my tent. You are welcome to help yourself before you…um, head to your own tent. It appears Gan-Pi will need to stand guard a bit longer."

"Thank you, my Rovet!" Birate sighs in relief. He moves to take the Scarlett's hand, but she'll has nothing to do with it. She starts walking toward the camp, eager to be done with the whole affair. Birate doesn't move.

"Birate." Maldinado says. "Gan-Pi won't wait long."

"Oh, right." Birate hurries after her.

Maldinado watches little Birty stumble up the hill. Firelight from the camp illuminates the sky, darkness is becoming more noticeable. He turns to continue his descent until blood grass is brushing his knees. In the moments before nightfall the blood grass is a deep red, almost black. These are his Adarian brothers. Warriors who have fallen before him. He runs his palms over the stalks. Darkness settles around him. He kneels, allows the blood grass to caress his face; breathes in the dusty smell of the field. He looks up into the night sky, raises his arms, and prays to the Sphere.

There's a rustling in the field. He's not alone. Little Birty, again?

"Who's there?" Maldinado demands.

Silence. Birate would have answered. An animal would have run. An enemy freezes.

"Who are you?" Maldinado reaches for his sword. "Show yourself!"

More rustling. Then a full rush. Maldinado rolls away

and waits. Silence. The blood grass is stiff against his cheeks. He can feel the other's presence, but he can't see him.

Movement! The outline of a figure less than three yards away.

Maldinado charges. The figure rises up, sword at the ready, but the battle is over quickly. The stranger falls with a groan. He's dead.

A brief search reveals the red cloak of a Worshiper of Morlac.

Maldinado lifts the body into position over his shoulder, and walks back toward the campfires of the Adarian 45th, back up the hill, his sword still drawn. He finds Hintor with a group of Adarians all gathered around a game of 5-Ruby. The Rovet parts the crowd as he heaves the body into the midst of his warriors.

"Assassins. Spread out and search the perimeter. If there's more I want them dead."

THE ADOW

The warriors of the Adarian 45th have an overbearing air of confidence. Not surprising. I've heard all about their exploits. How they squelched the riots in Kiel. Broke through the gates of Quel. Captured Gubyer, the traitor, by tracking him down in the Nelic Mountains. Then there's Adarian, hero of Ire, who was a Rovic of the Adarian 45th before he served as First Etabli. But the stories only describe their adventures. They fail to accurately depict these warriors.

They're giants, every one of them, and they walk with an effortless, though calculated, gait. Their hands rest comfortably upon the hilts of their sheathed swords. Those who walk past me bow without ever lowering their gaze, less a show of respect as it is a proclamation of their status within the Adowian Army. Definitely overbearing. But they do provide a sense of security. Even Faunride, walking in front of me, appears clumsy in comparison.

"I sent word to the Madar." Faunride reports, his dark eyes flickering from side to side watchfully, admiringly, as he walks. "He has made preparations for our arrival."

"Who is the Madar?" Ayson asks, walking behind me, as usual.

"Maldinado. He's young, but recently decorated and well respected by his warriors, many of whom owe him their lives."

"A Madar?"

Ayson voices my own curiosity. Madar is one of the few positions in the Adowian Army that honors blood over skill. The worst Madars, those who are stupid enough to give orders, are murdered by their own warriors. They're a political headpiece ignored by everyone.

"From what I understand, Maldinado serves as both Madar and Rovet." Faunride concludes.

Rovet? Impressive.

I glance back at Ayson. "Why haven't you recruited him for the Adowian Guard?"

Ayson avoids a pile of dung, walks around it, delaying his response.

I press the issue. "When was the last time a warrior from the Adarian 45th served in the Adowian Guard?"

"Not since Lio was First Etabli, my Adow." Faunride responds.

"Tasa Ro!"

Faunride cringes at my cursing, his traditions interfering with the reality of his Adow. He'll get over it. At this particular moment I don't feel like coddling his expectations.

"No wonder we're in this mess." Your mess, mother. Are you listening?

"What mess?" Ayson asks. I can't tell if he's serious or just clueless.

God of Another World: The Adow

"Look at them, Ayson." I acknowledge the self-indulgent bow of three warriors, one of whom carries the banner of the Adarian 45th. Not carrying it as much as walking with hallowed purpose. "I wouldn't have to worry about assassins if these warriors served in the Guard!"

I've said too much. I can see the hurt on Faunride's face. "I'm sorry, Faunride." That's all I can manage. He needs words of encouragement, but I don't have any at the moment.

The Madar's tent is located in the center of the encampment. It's scarlet and rectangular. Their banner flaps tauntingly atop each tent post, six on either side with three larger banners in the middle. I decide their air of confidence is mostly arrogance.

After Faunride announces my presence to the guards, I enter the tent through a scarlet curtain. The material is rough, a heavy canvas fraying around the edges. Probably the same tent they've always used.

"My Adow!"

The greeting is a chorus, perfectly timed by sixty-two warriors who stand at attention on either side of a gold runner. Striking. And they're wearing their ornamental armor, designed by the Adarian artist, Beaug. I was hoping they would. It's always been my favorite. Silver plates attached to chain mail. Black leather drawn tight around the body. Two emerald discs, one on the shoulder and one on the hip. Strips of green silk. Silver helmets with an emerald carving of Adarian, hero of Ire. I've seen it in Adarian parades, but I've never been this close. Stunning. The warriors bow without lowering their gaze.

An annoying lack of respect!

More than that, they're judging my escort, measuring them. No, they weren't taken from your ranks. No, they aren't Adarian. Don't blame me!

Faunride announces my presence, but I'm suddenly distracted by the total lack of decoration. The outside of the tent is clearly that of a Madar, but there is nothing inside to support such a distinction. And there are bedrolls behind the warriors! Is he letting these warriors sleep in his tent?

There's a table of food, mostly eaten. A barrel of wine sits between each bedroll, one of which serves as the tether pole for a black goat. She is nibbling frantically at her rope. I don't blame her. Stories of adventure aren't the only tales I've heard about the Adarian 45th. There's also the goats.

At the end of the gold runner I see their Madar. He's seated upon a wooden throne. A silver throne is customary, dear Madar. Hell, I've never even *seen* a wooden throne.

Maldinado rises. "It's with honor that I vacate my throne. May it be worthy of your presence."

If I wanted to sit on a piece of wood I'd climb a tree! I hold my tongue, forcing my most gracious smile.

He has long, black hair and a growing beard. Rigid facial structure. Gray, ice-like eyes. He's taller than Ayson, a thick neck that hints at the physique beneath his armor. He's actually wearing Armor! I've never known any Madar to wear armor. He approaches and kneels before me even as the First Etabli takes an unconscious step back.

"Why aren't you wearing the customary dress of a Madar?" Not that I mind him wearing Beaug's armor, it fits him well, but we all have our duties. Something he's obviously forgotten.

"I find armor to be more useful in battle, my Adow." His voice resonates through the tent. No wonder he inspires these warriors. "If it offends you…"

"What's your name?" Why did I ask that? I already know his name. Stay focused!

God of Another World: The Adow

"Maldinado."

"Does it have a meaning?"

"It means *wrath of the Sphere*."

Of course it does. He serves in the Adarian 45th, after all. His mother wouldn't dream of naming her son something that meant *gutted toad*.

"We have come to speak with the warrior who killed the would-be assassin," Ayson says.

Exactly! Why am I even speaking to this arrogant Madar?

Maldinado looks up at the First Etabli. "I'm the warrior you seek."

Damn! Anyone but him.

I draw my sword and touch the blade to his head. "May the Sphere be with you."

"And keep you in His light." He responds.

Faunride removes Maldinado's helmet. I've never been a fan of kissing cold metal. I sheath my sword and take Maldinado's head into my hands, leaning down to kiss him on the forehead. His hair is soft, like grain spilling out of my hand.

I have the sudden urge to devour him.

Sometimes I hate being the Adow. Sometimes I don't.

"May the Sphere be with you." I manage to avoid holding his hair to my cheeks, a poor display during such a ceremony. I lick my lips instead. Force myself to back away. Damn these warriors!

"And keep you in His light." He stands, towering above me.

That's it, time to leave.

"The Adarian 45th requests the honor of being the first to enter Dragon's Torment," Maldinado states.

I've known a hundred Madars, never one so eager

to enter battle...to die for their Adow...for a lie. *Oh, Maldinado, did I mention it's a story about a tiger!*

"We don't know what we face in the Torment," Ayson says.

"I've heard rumor we'll find Morlac. They say he's waiting for us."

I nod in acknowledgement. "I've heard similar rumors." It's about the only thing I hear, these days. *Oh, another thing you should know about me Maldinado, I can't hear the Sphere.*

"Then it's vital you send your finest warriors with the first assault." The Adarian warriors salute with pride as their Madar continues. "We've already defeated one of Morlac's worshipers. We have earned this position of honor."

And you're just arrogant enough to make the request. I decide I don't like Maldinado. "Such an honor doesn't come at the request of a Madar," I say in an elevated tone I learned from my mother. "It's *given* by the Adow. You would do well to remember your title, Madar! And even better to remember mine."

Maldinado bows deeply, again without lowering his gray eyes. "Forgive me, my Adow," he says with mock humility.

"The honor is yours." *Why did I say that? Tasa Ro! I should be cutting off his head not granting his request. Stay focused! On his gray eyes...*

I leave before he can make another request. The air is much cooler outside.

God of Another World: The Adow

Dsal Tiger

The figure of Dsal Tiger varies greatly depending upon the dallic where the taggle was born, ranging from Kiel where he is portrayed as white with black stripes, to Ire where he is described as being all black, more panther-like. This tale originated in the Caduum dallic, as a warning to those boys who would dream of escaping to a better life in the Torment. As such, the figure of Dsal Tiger is described as having two red eyes. His fur is white, and he has a single black stripe—a scar on his left side reaching from shoulder to hindquarters. It should also be noted that this traditional telling does not include the rabbit, a popular addition more recently.

The tale begins: Listen to these warnings, and may Dsal guide you to the Sphere.
- DK Vel

Dsal Tiger walks through a valley in Dragon's Torment where he has tracked the five wolves. Many have sought the wolves and never returned.

The bear is dead.

The lion is lost.

The owl has fled.

But Dsal Tiger remains. He looks around. Sniffs the air.

Continues carelessly, loudly, breaking sticks as he walks. The sound echoes throughout the valley.

A falcon hears the noise from overhead. "Flee this valley," it shrieks. "The Kul approaches."

"Have you seen the wolves?" Dsal Tiger calls, but the falcon flies away without another word.

Dsal Tiger doesn't flee. He's thirsty. The rain taunts him from a distance. He seeks a river, a lake–dew drops suspended from leaves, but there is nothing to quench his thirst. Finally, at the top of a mountain, above timberline, he finds a lake. He runs to its edge, lowering his head to drink. The water is cold as it travels through his body.

A fish appears, a small ripple within the waves created by Dsal Tiger's insatiable lapping. "Run from these waters. The Kul approaches."

"Have you seen the wolves?" Dsal Tiger asks, water dripping from the white fur around his mouth, but the fish is gone.

Dsal Tiger doesn't run. He's tired. He moves deeper into the Torment in search of a comfortable spot to rest, eventually coming upon a cave. He curls up, falls asleep beside a large rock.

The cave is filled with bats. "Leave this cave," they squeak. "The Kul approaches."

Dsal Tiger awakens to the sound of bats leaving the cave. "Have you seen the wolves?" he asks sleepily, but none of the bats turn at his question, so Dsal Tiger resumes his slumber.

There is the roar of a bear.

And the roar of a lion.

But neither bear nor lion appear. Their roars echo from within the Kul, a creature of wind and shadow–a creature now standing at the mouth of the cave. The Kul has come!

God of Another World: The Adow

Dsal Tiger is awake.

The roar of the bear fades. And that of the lion. Another sound, barely perceptible, is all that remains of the owl. "Who?"

Dsal Tiger feels the fur on his spine rise. He growls at the Kul, raises his paw in warning. The Kul is undeterred. Dsal Tiger lunges with a roar, but the creature of wind and shadow consumes him. He is gone, a lingering echo from within the Kul.

Don't enter the Torment. The Kul approaches!

ADARIAN

THE ADOW

The Adarian Greeting Rituals—my first as Adow. It's a test, a rite of passage, so I go over each stage of the ritual in my mind exactly how Troq taught them to me. The phrasing is very important, and the delivery. The Adarians will perceive any hesitation as a sign of weakness.

"The Adarians worship the Sphere, the Adow, and their traditions," Troq used to say, *"but the Adow is the only one they criticize."*

I don't blame them. The Adow have given them plenty of reason for complaint. This road we follow is the most obvious example, a lingering eyesore commissioned by my great grandmother. We reached the Adarian Road nine days ago. One day it may extend all the way to Yenul, but the process of paving the road with marble has long-since come to a halt. It seems my great grandmother forgot to account for the amount of marble it would actually take to complete the road. All of the marble quarries surrounding Adarian were exhausted before the third winter, and they've been searching for a new supply source ever since. Why wouldn't the Adarians criticize their Adow?

It's a fair exchange, I suppose—their loyalty gives them the right to pass judgment. I'd rather they didn't whisper, of course, but we all have our secrets. I have mine. *Come join me on a quest to find the Five Arms of the Sphere.* But there's no end to this quest. In that way I suppose I'm building my own marble road. I'm no better than my great grandmother.

Faunride stirs me from my thoughts, his dark face highlighting the whiteness of his eyes. "A rider approaches, First Etabli."

"The Greeting Rituals." Ayson says.

I nod. The rite of passage has begun. My hands are sweating. "I'll need Aiya."

"My Adow." Faunride bows and heads toward the supply caravan in search of my handmaiden. His galloping horse clamors upon the marble road.

"Who are you sending to Adarian as the Gift of Protection?" Ayson asks.

We've already had this discussion, but apparently he wants to have it again. "Nothing's changed. I'm sending Teyo."

"Teyo is a strong warrior," Ayson agrees. "But I was hoping you'd reconsider and send Faunride."

"Faunride belongs with his Adow." The fact is he's all that remains of my life before I became the Adow. I know it's selfish, but all the same I have no intention of allowing him to leave. Besides, he doesn't want to leave me.

"He'll be dishonored if you don't send him. He's earned it, more so than Teyo."

"You mean he's the only one capable of protecting me?"

"I didn't say that." Ayson adjusts his breastplate. His

momentary silence heightens the clacking of hoofs against the marble. "Faunride deserves to go."

Yes, he deserves to go, so did Troq…but Troq is dead and I can't go through the Rituals without at least having Faunride. He'll understand. "Protecting his Adow is a greater honor than taking part in the Greeting Rituals. Something you would be wise to remember."

"The worshipers of Morlac won't attempt anything while the Adarians are around. They'd never make it through the city gates."

I'm not worried about assassins. Hell, I could use my sword against an assassin! Ayson doesn't understand. He isn't the one being judged, the one being tested with each Greeting. I need the Adarians to follow me. They have to join this quest! They have to believe I'm telling the truth, or everything is lost. "I'm sending Teyo!"

"As you command." Ayson removes his helmet, runs a cloth over his bald head, absorbing the sweat. Then he replaces the helmet and moves his horse behind mine so he can sulk, but I have other things to worry about, right now.

"Your hair!" Faunride arrives with Aiya. She hands me a wet cloth for my face.

"We don't have much time. Make me beautiful, Aiya." I scrub around my eyes, my cheeks, and throat. The cloth is streaked brown by the time I'm done washing my face.

Aiya moves from her horse to the back of mine, begins pulling at my windblown hair. She braided it this morning, but it was giving me a headache. I took it out as soon as she was out of sight. It's not like she didn't know I would do it. We've been arguing about my hair for ages.

A rider appears on the road ahead. He carries the banner of Gan, Overseer of Adarian: a green sphere with three white stripes on a white background. Troq told me the rider is always young, symbolizing hope and peace. He's escorted by two of my guards, Pwax and Og, their golden armor diffusing the silver gleam of the yearling's shield.

Aiya finishes my hair with a sigh meant to tell me she's not pleased, that it's the best she can do from the back of a horse. Fair enough. I'm the one who took the braid out. Tasa Ro! Why do I always make everything so difficult? She brushes the dust from my gown, cream velvet with a green braid, before returning to her horse.

"Almost ready." She rummages through a knitted sack to produce half a lemon. "This'll revive those cheeks."

She holds the lemon out for me to bite into, a sour warmth that coats my teeth, spreads a dryness across the inside of my upper lip. Cheeks withdraw from mouth. Eyes squint. My throat tingles as I swallow hard. Tasa Ro! "Thank you, Aiya."

Ayson motions the army to a halt as the rider approaches. Faunride positions himself on my left, close enough to touch, close enough to grab for his hand, but I resist the urge. He wouldn't let me if I tried. It's enough to have him beside me.

The Adarian rider is younger than me, sits tall in the saddle, the pride of Adarian already stiffening his back. He wears a white tunic and a brilliant green cloak decorated with silver thread. He bows with a practiced grace, his eyes never leaving mine. Dammit! Everything about him is perfect!

"Gan, Overseer of Adarian, greets his Adow with a blessing," the yearling declares. "The Sphere is with you, my Adow."

Here we go, "Gan has greeted me with hope and peace.

THE ADOW

Return under the banner of your Adow," my mouth feels twice as large. I'm over pronouncing every word. But I got them out, and I didn't forget a single word. Are you listening, Troq? I motion toward Valin who dutifully hands over the Adowian banner, a white sphere upon a golden background, in exchange for the banner of Gan.

The yearling bows. "May the Sphere be with you."

"And keep you in His light."

He leaves without escort. The first greeting is complete. I'm sweating as badly as Ayson. Tasa Ro, this dress is hot! "Aiya, the next gown!"

There are twenty-four greetings and, thankfully, five hours between each greeting. Ayson gives the order to make camp and by the time the second rider appears, Aiya has rebraided my hair to her satisfaction. Where would I be without her? A windblown disaster! She dresses me in a purple gown with exposed neck and shoulders, but I still can't breathe. Fortunately, I'm seated beneath the shade of a makeshift canopy so I'm no longer sweating. Now I'm shaking.

The second rider is old. Only the most decorated Adarian warriors are chosen for this task, but I don't recognize the rider who wears his medals with seasoned arrogance. He is in full ceremonial armor and his long gray hair is braided. He dismounts as he reaches the perimeter of the Adowian Guard. They escort him into my presence where he unsheathes his sword and falls to one knee–fully embracing my gaze…judging me.

"Gan, Overseer of Adarian, offers you his sword, my Adow." The warrior raises the sword hilt toward me.

My mouth is so dry! "Gan has lain down his defenses, and I offer the protection of the Adowian Army." …*in return*. I meant to say I offer the protection of the Adowian

Chad Michael Cox

Army in return, but it's too late. My first mistake.

I motion toward Teyo—not Faunride. Teyo exchanges swords with the warrior, mounts the Adarian's horse, and rides off toward the city.

As I watch him leave I realize my second mistake. I've forgotten an entire portion of the greeting which should have come before Teyo left. Dammit! "What is your name?" I ask the warrior who is still kneeling there waiting with a look of self-satisfaction.

"Daden."

"I am honored, Daden. Join my Guard and protect me with your life." And water, get me some water.

"It is I who am honored, my Adow." He rises, sheathes Teyo's sword, and moves to join my guards.

I look up at Faunride. I want to tell him I didn't forget the order of the Greeting on purpose, but he isn't looking at me. He's staring resolutely at the Adarian Road in front of my throne. He's staring at Teyo riding toward Adarian; a distant clatter.

I grab for his hand, but he avoids my grip. Of course he does. He won't permit himself to touch his Adow, not even when she needs him the most. "I need you beside me, Faunride." Please understand. That's the reason I sent Teyo. I can't do this without you.

"The honor is Teyo's, my Adow. He is a fine warrior." Faunride responds without lowering his gaze, his dark eyes as vacant as a deer's lying dead before the hunter. He is hurt. Perhaps I should have... No—he is *my* guardian.

"I need Aiya." That will help him get over the disappointment. Faunride would be lost without his duties. "And water!"

Faunride bows. "My Adow."

Ayson extends his hand dutifully, but I stand without

God of Another World: The Adow

his help. If Faunride refuses to touch me…if I can't be touched…I don't need Ayson, right now. I need Troq! But he isn't here. I head toward my tent. Preparations for the next greeting need to be made, and I need to bathe. I'm sweating, again! Ayson follows without a word.

~

Five hours later, the army is mounted and waiting as a rider approaches. Not just any rider, *the* rider. The only one I remember from my first trip to Adarian. She rides upon a horse of dark pink, almost purple, an inane color that, for her, seems majestic. Her robes are white and flow loosely in the wind. Her hair matches the horse, as though it were an extension of its mane. Her features are young, her skin pale and flawless. She rides bareback, her hands resting peacefully upon her legs, for there are no reins to guide the horse. The rider and the horse have been joined by the Sphere since the beginning of time. She is unchanged. Every feature is the same as it was the first time I saw her.

This is Inindu, sister of the Adow.

It is the horse who speaks. "Greetings, my Adow." The voice is a mixture of feminine harmony and the deep breaths of a warhorse. I'm fairly certain this is a goddess, or the next closest thing, but all I can think about is the sweat running down my arms and if she will notice how nervous I am. It doesn't help knowing Inindu has been alive since the beginning of time. How many of these rituals has she attended? She'll notice every mistake.

"Greetings, Inindu," I respond. "And blessings upon thee." Sweating, again! I hate ceremonies!

Inindu is neither horse nor topi; she is the spirit of both, and the soul of neither. She was also the lover of Adarian, hero of Ire. The same Adarian whom the Adow chose to serve as her First Etabli. The one who died in the arms of the Adow. If anyone has a reason to despise the Adow, it's Inindu. *But it wasn't me, Inindu. Don't blame me. I wasn't the Adow that chose Adarian. For that matter, I didn't even choose my own First Etabli!*

"I don't speak for Gan, though he would wish it otherwise." *That's not what she's supposed to say.* "I've never really liked the Greeting Rituals." Inindu doesn't even attempt to hide her irritation.

Her lack of interest in the ceremony is jarring, but it manages to calm my nerves to a degree. Nevertheless, acknowledging the fact that I would rather be doing something else, anything else, doesn't strike me as something an Adow would admit. "It's an old tradition, Inindu. One that brings comfort to old souls."

"The words of one so young…one day you'll come to understand that loneliness is the only comfort for old souls."

Faunride moves his horse a step closer, realizing the ceremony is off course, his sense of tradition no doubt conflicting with Inindu's complete disregard.

"I understand loneliness more than you know, Inindu." *I didn't mean to say that.*

She looks at Ayson. "Then the rumors are true?"

Ayson looks down at the road.

"Shall we continue with the greeting ritual?" I press.

"If you wish."

"I do."

"Very well. Gan, Overseer of Adarian, greets you with beauty; or rather he greets you with *my* beauty. As for Gan, he has not aged gracefully."

Then those rumors are also true. "Gan is blessed, regardless of his age. He has greeted me with beauty, and I offer beauty in return."

God of Another World: The Adow

THE ADOW

Ayson unsheathes his sword and moves his horse closer to me, raising a single strand of my black hair. He cuts it and rides forward to hand the strand to Inindu, avoiding her eyes…both sets of them. He's always been uncomfortable around her. He quickly sheathes his sword and returns to my side. Weapons make him uncomfortable, too.

"Will you join us at the Greeting Feast?" I ask. It would be good to talk with her when the conversation isn't dictated by ritual.

Inindu looks at Ayson. "Will you be at the feast, First Etabli?"

"I go wherever my Adow goes, Inindu."

"Yet you are here, now, before us." Inindu smiles. "Yes, I will attend. And I will go wherever you go, Ayson. We have much to discuss: Quel, marriage, heirs to the throne…"

"I would be honored by your presence, Inindu." Ayson lowers his gaze.

"I'm sure." Inindu turns. "My Adow."

I watch her leave, wishing she would stay. But she disappears over the horizon, signaling the start of the next greeting ritual. "I need Aiya."

Faunride bows, "My Adow."

~

During the Greeting Rituals, the Adarian Road is cleared and travelers are detained in both directions providing yet another reason for the Adarians to criticize me. No one likes to be delayed when they travel, let alone for five days. Five days of ceremony. Five days of sweating and bathing. I can't drink enough water! Turn away, Troq! I can barely function. All your training…

"A rider approaches, my Adow," Ayson announces.

It's midday of the fourth day. I set my plate down on the ground: seasoned boar with warm applesauce and greens,

Chad Michael Cox

mostly untouched because my stomach has been burning since the morning meal of pickled garlic, bread, and fried pork.

"I need a new cook." I take the last sip of wine before standing to face Aiya. I'm wearing a yellow and green gown. She hands me a cloth for my face then busies herself with my hair.

"Find me a new cook, Faunride."

"My Adow." He bows as the next ritual begins.

~

There's a new greeting every five hours. My tongue is sticking to my teeth, but somehow I manage to get through each ceremony. The last ritual takes place in front of the city gates. It's a beautiful sight! Why I'm forced to live in Yenul when there's a city like Adarian, is beyond me. The city that Beaug sculpted stretches the length of the horizon. Its walls are marble, every inch a sculpted image, and atop the walls are great statues of warriors engaged in endless battle. One of the images is of Adarian, hero of Ire, hanging onto the mast of a ship, leaning out from the walls, battling a sea serpent in the surrounding forest. Incredible! Even more so on a windy day when the forest sways with a sound that imitates the sea. Or at night, when the moon reflects off the marble figures. I used to sit in Troq's lap atop the city walls and stare at those figures for hours, fall asleep in his arms.

The entrance to the city is no less impressive. It's guarded by two marble figures, giants who sit upon their thrones on either side of a silver gate. One topi is female: slightly turned and lifting a large, open book. The other figure is heavily bearded, leaning forward in thought. They are framed by waterfalls that pool at the base of each statue. The two ponds have, over time, become an integral part of any visit to the city. Travelers, whether coming or going, throw a coin into the pool - one side for safe travels, the other for prosperity during their visit. Of course Gan, Overseer of Adarian, has placed guards at the gate to ensure this ritual continues; a subtle form of taxation the Adarians don't seem to mind paying. Impressive! If they tried that in Yenul I'd have a revolt. Or Lor–they'd never go for it in Lor.

The city gates are open before us and I can see Beaug's masterpiece just inside the entrance: a black marble sculpture of Adarian, hero of Ire. He lies dying in the arms of the Adow, or someone who is meant to represent the Adow. It's the only statue of the Adow whose face is not a mirror image of my own; of my mother. It's my favorite piece for that reason alone. Adarian's body is draped over the Adow's lap, one arm hanging, slipping away from her. Her cloak gathers around him, great swells of material that mimic his limp form. She cradles him in her arms, willing him to live. But there is nothing the Adow can do. We cannot restore life to the dying. I know. I've tried. Troq isn't coming back, and neither is Adarian.

A thousand Adarians line the marble road, gathered here to greet me–to judge me for themselves. Behind me, the Adowian Army awaits the signal telling them the Greeting Rituals are complete. Most of them will celebrate for the next several days, knowing it may be their last meal, their last drink, or their last lover. I can't help but forgive their anticipation. I am asking them to die for me. They deserve every ounce of joy.

A cheer arises from the city gates. "The Overseer, First Etabli." Faunride introduces the last greeting ritual. The Overseer lies in an open caravan, carried on the shoulders of eight topis.

Chad Michael Cox

Inindu was right. Gan is old, dreadfully old, even from this distance I can see the evidence of his poor health. His face looks as though it's being pulled downward by the unseen hands of the grave, leaving clumps of skin dangling from his jaw. His white hair is mostly gone, and what remains is unkempt. His body is bent and twisted, his belly bloated. He wears a white robe and leans awkwardly against the exposed torso of his lover, Erisyte, who himself is leaning against pillows.

"Welcome to Adarian, my dear Adow," he calls out in a faltering voice.

"I am honored, Gan. It is good to see you in such good health." I smile graciously.

The caravan comes to a stop. "It took them an hour to get me onto this contraption, my dear, and I had to bring Erisyte along just so I wouldn't fall off." I glance at the handsome topi who cradles Gan in his arms. Gan has many lovers, but Erisyte is known to be his only companion. "It will not take so long to get down, I think."

"May it take a thousand years," I respond.

He smiles. "You are kind, my Adow, but death carries a blade that even I cannot avoid."

I doubt he'll last another year. Then again, it's also possible he'll outlive me. I'm heading to Dragon's Torment, after all. Why shouldn't he outlive me? Hell, he's already outlived twelve previous Adow! Yes, I pray he does outlive me! Gan *is* the city of Adarian. He's the one who commissioned a young Beaug to sculpt the city, developed roads and sewage systems, recruited warriors from all over the land, encouraged and cultivated discourse among Adarian philosophers, created sport and games for the Adarian public, and built the only library in the land. He can't be

THE ADOW

replaced. I don't want to replace him. Not now, anyway. I have enough to worry about, and we have a greeting ritual to get through.

"You have greeted me with your presence, Gan. I offer my presence in return."

"I am honored, my Adow. Adarian celebrates your arrival." He gestures to his bearers. "I will escort you to your quarters, and then to the courtyard for the Greeting Feast."

The crowd erupts in celebration. That's it. I've done it, Troq!

a taggle's tale

As told by a taggle woman in front of a marble statue, the only known likeness of Hintor. The telling was well rehearsed, and she utilized the statue well, at times pointing toward it to emphasize the moment. She turned an obvious distraction into a silent facilitator–a new technique which I must admit is worth exploring. Her words were not as crisp as an old man desires, but the audience seemed to respond well enough. Her name is Mistan. She is my granddaughter. She speaks in the manner of all taggles, for our story is a journey we share. May the Sphere forgive our mother and remember our father, as revealed in Dsal's vision.

- DK Vel

"It's been a long time, Nataline." Hintor twirls Maldinado's sister around in his arms, barely missing the heads of the two yearlings standing beside her, but he is quick to kneel and turn his attention to them. "And who are these two beauties? Are you taking in strangers, again?"

The tallest, Kaletine, drops the basket she is carrying and gives Hintor a tight hug around the throat. The other yearling, Belur, crashes into his side, causing all three to fall onto the marble Adarian Road. The warrior feigns a counter-attack, roaring and gathering the yearlings into his arms, squeezing them until they giggle. He gives both of them a kiss.

"What did you bring us, Uncle Hintor?" Belur searches his cloak for hidden treasure.

"Belur." Nataline scolds softly. "It's enough that Hintor has returned from battle."

"No it's not." Kaletine folds her arms and stares down at Hintor from atop the warrior's chest, daring him to refuse her a gift. "Uncle Hintor always brings us something, but he hides it. Where did you hide our present, Uncle Hintor?"

"I've forgotten where I put them."

"See, mommy." Belur intones. "Uncle Hintor did too bring us something."

"Yes, Belur. It appears he did." Nataline retrieves the basket Kaletine was carrying. "And we've brought him something, too. Let him up. The bread is growing stale while you three roll around on the ground."

Reluctantly, the yearlings allow Hintor to stand. They lift up his cloak and run around him searching for their gift. Hintor reaches for the basket. "Maldinado said you would bring bread."

Nataline positions herself between Hintor and the basket. "And where is my brother?"

"Praying."

"You could learn from his example."

Belur sneaks behind her mother, grabs a fresh loaf of bread, and hands it to Hintor. The warrior smiles broadly as he bites into the sourdough.

"That won't help you, Belur." Nataline says. "Your Uncle Hintor enjoys torturing the two of you."

"Give us a clue." Kaletine pleads.

Hintor swallows and lowers himself until he is staring directly into the eyes of the two yearlings. "Where did I hide them last time?"

"In a barrel." The yearlings answer in unison.

"In a barrel…well, it's not there this time." Hintor takes another bite.

"You're hopeless." Nataline says, but her daughters are deep in thought, pondering the location of their treasure.

Hintor stands and resumes walking. "Maldinado tells me the same thing."

All around them, Adarian warriors are greeting the family and friends they left behind. It's the Tenth Greeting, the only one in which the Adow does not participate. Five hours reserved solely for the Adarian warriors returning home. Hintor, Nataline, and her daughters travel through the crowd, eventually leaving the marble road in favor of the bloodgrass hills where the Adarian 45th has made a temporary camp. The expanse of the horizon is covered with tents, wagons, horses, and warriors awaiting entrance to the city.

"The wagons!" Kaletine guesses.

Hintor shakes his head. His mouth is full of bread.

"Your tent!" Belur shouts.

"Not even close." Hintor shoves the last of the bread into his mouth and reaches for another loaf.

Nataline adjusts the basket, moving it out of his reach. "Save some for Maldinado."

Hintor leads them through the maze of tents even as the yearlings check behind every wagon wheel, bale of hay, and animal trough. The bloodgrass lays flat throughout the camp, trampled and shredded over the past two days. Barrels of wine are everywhere, a gift from the Adow. A crowd gathers around each one.

Hintor motions to the taggle boy who follows him, DK Vel. The taggle races to fill a goblet. He returns a moment later, and Hintor drinks the wine like a horse sloshing through a river. The wine runs freely down his chin onto his black and red doublet.

"Manners, Hintor." Nataline reproaches him. "Adarians are nothing without their manners."

Hintor finishes the wine with an exaggerated exhale. "Indeed, but I am from Plenrid."

"Yes, but our children will be Adarians."

Hintor stops walking. "Our children?"

"Kanbis has been dead long enough." Nataline says as she passes Hintor. "You may court me if you wish."

Hintor wipes the wine from his mouth. The yearlings return from another fruitless search.

"Give us another clue, Uncle Hintor!" Kaletine demands. She is not as patient as her sister, Belur. She's older. Old enough to have been adversely affected by her father's death.

Hintor looks at the yearling with sudden apprehension. This could be his daughter. She's waiting for him to respond. Belur hugs his leg, sits on his foot in position to ride as he walks. He looks past the yearlings and stares after Nataline. This could be *his* family! His grin is wider than the scar across his nose.

"Find the goat." Hintor says.

The yearlings take off in a dash of delight, running past their mother who is telling them to stop running. Hintor forces his legs to work, moving forward until he has caught up to Nataline. He walks beside her with casual flare.

"Will you marry me?" He proposes.

"That is yet to be determined." Nataline states.

Hintor stops walking for the second time.

~

Maldinado embraces Kaletine and Belur in a bear hug. Then he pulls them back, abruptly. Looks at them sternly. "Have you been helping your mother?"

Both nod, sheepishly looking to their mother for confirmation.

"More than not." Nataline offers. "Kaletine looks after the horses, and Belur is starting to cook."

"And your prayers?" Maldinado eyes them suspiciously. Again they nod.

"You should try my pudding!" Belur says excitedly.

"I can't wait!" Maldinado enwraps them again before standing to give his sister a kiss on the forehead.

"Maldinado," Kaletine searches the tent. "Where's your goat?"

The Madar looks at Hintor who is standing just inside the tent. His friend holds his arms up in mock confusion. "You hid their gifts on the goat?" Maldinado shakes his head with disapproval then points toward the back of the tent, an unlit cloak of shadows. "He's grazing in the fields with the other goats."

The yearlings sprint out of the tent toward the fields beyond the camp. Hintor turns to follow. "I better go with them. I may have tied the key around his neck a little too tight."

Maldinado looks down at his younger sister. Her black hair is long and braided. She stares back at him with warm, brown eyes that have always reminded him of aged wood. "You look more like Breline every time I see you."

"She wanted to come." Nataline hands her brother a loaf of bread, sets the basket down on a barren table.

"How is our mother?" Maldinado bites into the loaf,

God of Another World: The Adow

memories of home rise to the surface.

"Opinionated as ever." Nataline sits down on her brother's wooden throne. Maldinado takes another bite of bread. "She doesn't want you to go on this quest."

"Do you?" Maldinado asks.

"I've never told you what to do."

Maldinado finishes the bread, rummages through the basket for another loaf. "Things are different, now. I won't watch another Adow die."

"I know. I told her you have to go." Nataline watches her brother eat. It's the least she can do for him. Cook. He sends her every ounce of gold he receives for serving in the Adarian Army. He's as much a father to her daughters as Kanbis ever was while he lived. "You're a fine warrior, Maldinado. You have to go–I won't hold it against you."

"Dragon's Torment doesn't frighten me. It's Breline I'm worried about."

"You should be–it's been six years since you were home. And don't think she didn't notice the other warriors came back after Quel. If it hadn't been for your letters we'd have thought you were dead."

"I couldn't leave the Adow." Maldinado walks over to his sister, brings her to her feet, then sits in the throne behind her with a grin.

She slugs him in the chest. Several times. He grabs her and twists her until she's pinned under his arms.

"Are you coming to the Greeting Feast?" He asks.

She struggles to free herself of his grip. Finally, he relents. She stands and adjusts her dark blue gown. "I haven't decided."

Kaletine runs into the tent waving a golden key. "Where's the chest?"

Maldinado stands with a smile, pointing to the wooden

throne. "Under my seat."

Hintor enters the tent carrying Belur on his back.

"Did you find it?" Belur shouts.

Hintor lowers her to the ground so she can run to her sister's side. Kaletine lifts the throne seat and removes a small wooden chest. Inside, the yearlings find a pair of emerald earrings—one for each of them.

Hintor watches their eyes light up with wonder even as his gaze drifts toward Nataline.

a taggle's tale

As first spoken by a taggle man outside the Adarian castle. The gathered crowd was riotous, pushing and jostling for position until at last the man sought an elevated platform. Thus, he told his tale from atop the castle wall, shouting loudly for all topis and taggles to hear. His movements were minimal, for the moment required little more than the words he spoke to garner the attention of his audience. When they were still, he began his tale. His name was Tuloo, chosen to serve Gan, Overseer of Adarian. He spoke in the manner of all taggles, for our story is a journey we share. May the Sphere forgive our mother and remember our father, as revealed in Dsal's vision.

- DK Vel

Masks disappear and reappear as dancers turn their heads. The fixed emotions worn by the masqueraders shift and move like hunters among the trees. A flash of white is removed, and grinning gold appears; red glitter is quickly hidden by a purple feather. Hands rise with the music and feet skip in rhythm. Diamond eyes wink at black faces, and painted stripes blend with velvet tassels. The laughter is mixed with conversation, and only the feasting slows the wine.

This is the Greeting Feast.

Hintor stands in the crowd, searching for the mask of the Red Death; it is completely red, with no decoration. He doesn't know who's behind the mask, but the identity of the topi doesn't matter. It's what the mask of the Red Death will *bring* that concerns Hintor the most: belladonna root. In small doses, this powder is Adarian's drug of choice. Of course, an overdose will prove lethal. The victim breaks out in a red rash, their pupils dilate, they hallucinate, lose their sense of balance, and collapse. Their heart rate increases, then slows, and stops. The mask of the Red Death attends every feast and festival in Adarian. A simple exchange of gold for powder occurs, and the mask of the Red Death disappears.

Hintor moves through the crowd. He's wearing a full mask, white with gold stenciling and rustic creases at the eyes and nostrils; only his lips are exposed. Jagged black lines give the impression that the mask was once shattered and then pieced back together. He sees the mask of the Red Death moving slowly through conversation circles. The exchange is unseen, but Hintor sees the latest client discreetly pour a white powder into his wine. The mask of the Red Death vanishes…then it appears again beside Hintor, as though seeing the mask was enough to attract its presence. The act of searching. Hintor hands the topi a pouch of gold and receives four tubes of powder, three more than the traditional purchase. The mask of the Red Death disappears, and Hintor knows he will not see it again.

His attention shifts as the Adow and her First Etabli enter the courtyard. Their masks are the most recognizable of the celebration, for they have been the same since the inception of the feast. They are surrounded by a crowd thirty heads deep, most of whom have political aspirations. The Overseer will soon be dead, after all, and an heir has not been appointed. It's in the best interests of those in attendance to seek an audience with the Adow.

She wears a simple white gown and a mask of gold and white, the gold encircling the Adow's eyes as though it were a second mask. Gold lips and fashioned spikes with dangling bells complete the disguise. The First Etabli is a sun god. He wears a black robe, leather gloves, and tight fitting black coif under a raised cowl. His polished bronze mask is like fire. Flames extend wildly from his eyes. The mask consumes his head, complete with molded lips and sculpted chin.

Hintor hides the tubes of belladonna root, and dips his goblet into the closest barrel. Wine runs and falls from his metal goblet like blood streaking a sword. He drinks the wine…slowly. Nataline wants him to drink with manners.

Manners!

He refills the goblet, buries his nose in the wine in his haste to consume it. He's always wanted to marry Nataline, but now that she's given him permission… He fills the goblet again and surveys the room, spots Maldinado a few yards away. His friend is standing alone, dressed entirely in gold with a simple golden mask around his eyes and nose.

Hintor fills another goblet and joins his friend. "I feel the need to get drunk."

Maldinado raises a toast. "To the Adow!"

"To your sister!" Hintor counters, but Maldinado can't hear above the crowd.

They drink heartily.

Hintor lowers his mask and takes the Madar's cup,

hands him two tubes of belladonna root in exchange. "A gift from a friend. I'll get some more wine."

Maldinado conceals the drug in the pocket of his doublet. Then he is pulled onto the dance floor. His partner has dark pink hair and a matching half-moon mask that lassos her exposed right eye. topi-Inindu does not say a word. Her voice, Inindu-horse, is standing off to the side. Watching. Listening to the conversations that surround her.

"…and now I have come…"

"…most of it began to surface…"

"…and take off this mask."

"…a new law that is itself a revision of the previous…"

"…children sleeping, but I guess I can't worry about the flowers, and in the morning it will all…"

"…cold night…"

The conversations cease as Gan enters the courtyard. The Overseer of Adarian, host of this celebration, wears a mask of blue silk that forms a wave at the top of his head. His face is a pin cushion of blue beads, as though raindrops are suspended around his eyes, covering his brow. He wears a pair of large, heart-shaped earrings that extend downward in a shower of crystal and silver.

Hintor takes a gulp of wine, approaches Maldinado, and slips between his friend and Inindu. The exchange of dancing partners is seamless, leaving Maldinado to search for another. His eyes fall on the topis beside Gan. Maldinado supposes most to be his lovers, but some of them are female. One of them wears a full mask with gold leaves and blue jewels. He moves toward her, scratches his upper lip, extends his hand to her, and bows.

She accepts his invitation. Grabs him. Nails jabbing into

his fingers. Her energy overwhelms him. They are dancing before either have the chance to speak. She moves her body close to him. Then away. She spins around him, raises her arms. The Madar embraces his partner, places his hands on her back, her black hair brushes against the back of his hands. She collapses. Her arms move around him. Maldinado presses his cheek to her skin, smelling the creams and oils–the sweat on her body like warm spices.

He closes his eyes.

She stiffens. He releases her with a twirl. The gold leaves and blue jewels of her mask stop spinning and she returns to him, but he keeps his distance. Only their hands are touching. He stares into her eyes, outlined in dark tones– she raises them! Invites him to pull her closer. He wants to–he wants to feel her body against him once more, but their dance has come to an end. Their fingers embrace.

He holds her a moment too long.

The dance demands they exchange partners.

The music stops.

"I hope you are not my sister," Maldinado says softly.

The stranger shakes her head. "I don't have any brothers."

The music resumes.

Maldinado takes her into his arms. "What is your name?"

"Don't ask me my identity."

"Ah! So we're playing the parts of Tenush and Gieel." Maldinado leads her slowly, wraps her gently with his arm.

"*Misdeblue* is an ancient tale." She rests her head against his chest. "I've always hated the ending."

"You prefer tragic endings?" Maldinado asks.

"Life prefers tragedy," she states with a sigh. "I've seen too many deaths to think otherwise."

"You're not from Adarian." Maldinado places his nose and lips against her hair. It's wet with sweat, a moist smell textured with oils.

"Why do you say that?"

"Because Adarian is a city of hope and joy—look around you." The Madar motions toward the masquerade.

"I see strangers unwilling to reveal their identities."

"I'm not a stranger. Do you wish to know my name?" Maldinado pauses. "I'll tell you anything you want."

"No." She looks into his eyes. "I don't want to know your name. Not tonight."

The music changes tempo.

"Why do you grow a beard?" she asks.

"I'm headed to Dragon's Torment. It's a way to stay warm." Maldinado extends his partner to the right. Brings her close.

"It seems everyone is heading to the Torment."

"We follow the Adow."

"So does my father."

"Then he is honored," Maldinado turns her until they are dancing back to back.

"He is *not* honored."

"What happened?"

She steps away. Returns. Their arms extend and lock. "You promised me hope and joy. Let's change the subject."

"You must come from Kiel." Maldinado closes his eyes. Embraces her movements. Feels her body against him.

"Why do you say that?"

"I know the warriors from Kiel. They're all sad."

She seems amused. "You're trying to figure out who I am."

Maldinado opens his eyes. "I'm hoping you'll join me for the Toast of Sark."

God of Another World: The Adow

"I have many suitors."

"A kiss from you is worth the pursuit," Maldinado counters.

"Then I'm yours to pursue." She moves with the music to another partner.

~

Dancers move in circles and lines. Crowds mingle around trees, barrels of wine. The courtyard is a painting of colors that swirl and stop and blend. Inindu-horse turns from her study of the Adow to a topi who is wearing the most absurd mask of the evening, complete with tongue sticking out. The paint on the tip of the tongue is chipped.

"She's drawing quite a crowd."

"I've never understood this celebration," the tongued one says.

"It gives Adarians a reason to drink wine…something I've noticed your mask doesn't allow you to do," Inindu-horse replies.

"It keeps me sober. What it's intended to do."

"It keeps you single, too. You don't have to worry about kissing anyone for the Toast of Sark."

"I have you."

Inindu-horse shakes her mane. "My heart belongs to Adarian."

"Of course. I didn't mean to suggest…"

"This is the only place we were permitted to see each other. I'm sure you can figure out how we accomplished that."

The tongued-one nods in agreement. "The masks have many uses."

"Which is all you need to know about this ridiculous celebration." Inindu notices Gan in the middle of the courtyard. He raises his goblet, gulps down the wine. "Gan will find any reason to have a feast."

"He's old. If anyone deserves to enjoy his last days, it's the Overseer."

"It won't be long," Inindu says. "He's the only living topi who knew my Adarian, but his mind grows weak. His memories are fading."

"He looks healthy enough."

"You're a poor liar. The truth is Gan is dying and he's grown rather boring," Inindu says. She finds the Adow in the crowd. "It's about time I leave this city. I think I'll journey to Dragon's Torment. Watching a thousand warriors die is much more interesting than watching an old Overseer meet his end."

~

The assassin watches the taggles as they take food and wine to the Adow. His plan will work. She's the only topi at the celebration who isn't supplying her own wine. He imagines it has always been this way. Worshippers flocking to her, making a mockery of themselves. He finds the masks suddenly transformed, fools bowing before the deceiver they call the Adow—seeking honor they'll never find.

Only Morlac can provide peace.

The assassin dips his goblet into the wine barrel, empties a tube of belladonna root into the wine. Drinks it gone. He fondles the remaining four tubes he's saved for the Adow, follows a taggle out of the courtyard.

The Toast of Sark is near. The Adow will kiss her First Etabli, and drink from a golden goblet. The assassin follows the taggle through a dark tunnel. He can feel, or rather see, the effects of the belladonna root. Faces appear in the shadows. Strangers—twisted, mutilated faces shimmering in greens and blues. They're wearing masks. Laughing. Whispering. Arms reach for him. The assassin waves at them. They disappear in a fog.

He laughs. It's been a long time since he's felt the effects of the belladonna root. Floating on the outskirts of these hallucinations is a taggle. A piece of reality that pulls the Worship of Morlac forward. He follows the taggle. Turns and follows. Walls liquefy. The assassin touches them, pulls his hand back. It's dripping with water.

The taggle is getting farther away. The assassin is lying on the ground. He pulls himself to his feet, follows the taggle. He's falling toward a lit room, clings to the walls to slow his descent. It's no use. He crashes into a wooden table. The room swirls. Images of meat and fruits. Bread dances with knives, pots, and bowls.

There is more than one taggle in the room, one of them is a boy. The assassin can't make out their faces. He doesn't care. He leans on the table, waits for the effects of the drug to fade.

"Out!" he screams. "Leave me!"

"Go away!" The assassin shouts.

The taggles leave, an eruption of commotion. The assassin is alone, free to search for the bottle of wine reserved for the Toast of Sark. It's the best wine—served only to the Adow, only during the Toast of Sark. He finds the bottle on a shelf. He smells the sweet pear wine.

He takes a drink. And another.

He pours four tubes of belladonna root into the bottle, and corks it once more. Moments later, the assassin has vanished.

~

Maldinado holds the long white ribbon that allows him

to choose his partner. The ribbon dances. He knows who he wants. He's lost her three times, but the Madar won't lose her again. He scans the masqueraders, pausing at every golden face. They're mocking him, hiding her. There! Their eyes make contact. She awaits her captor. Maldinado wraps the ribbon around her waist.

"I've figured out who you are," he says.

She laughs. "I'm a star above the clouds."

"No! You're both the storm and the rain."

She judges him—stares at the gold thread encircling his grey eyes. His black beard. "And you're a tree consumed by lightning!"

She spins away and out of the ribbon.

He wraps her again. The music starts. The dance has begun.

Maldinado grins. "Maybe I'm a painter eager to travel the land, or a herald."

"If you could be anyone, who would you be?" The ribbon slides over her shoulder and around her back. She moves closer to Maldinado.

"The First Etabli." Maldinado looks at the sun-god mask of the First Etabli. He stands beside the Adow, always beside the Adow.

"Why?"

"Wouldn't you want to be the Adow?"

"No." The disavowal is flat and convincing.

"Ah. Then who *would* you be?"

She smiles. Turns. "The storm and the rain."

He kneels, moves the ribbon over her feet. Twirls it upward around her body. "I can see you as Inindu."

"She's beautiful. I would gladly be Inindu."

"She's sad," he says. "Forever lonely, yet never alone."

God of Another World: The Adow

She stops dancing, looks into his eyes. Quickly resumes the dance. "You never said why you would want to be the First Etabli."

Maldinado relents. "There is no greater honor than to die protecting the Adow."

She steps away. Returns. "And what if you failed to protect her?"

He holds her firmly against his chest. "I would not fail."

"Then you are a fool." She grabs the ribbon and wraps it around his waist. "The First Etabli has already failed to protect the Adow. Remember Quel?"

"I was there." He moves in step with her. "Adarian warriors have a saying: we cannot alter the path of the sun, but we can embrace its journey, and trust the ending will be more beautiful than the beginning." He motions toward the Adow. "I failed to protect her once. I won't fail again." He takes the ribbon from her, wraps their wrists together.

She looks at the Adow. "I see a mask that can't be removed, a yearling who's lost her way."

"You're wrong," Maldinado says gently. He unwraps her wrists. "I've looked into her eyes. She isn't lost."

The music crescendos. Maldinado takes the ribbon in both hands, extending it as though it were a stick. She grips the middle. They walk in a circle. She ducks under, comes up into his arms. Raises the ribbon and moves away. The music ends. Maldinado wraps the ribbon around her waist one final time. A gong sounds.

"Where are your suitors?" he asks. "It's the Toast of Sark."

"Only one remains," is her coy reply.

"Then I'll get us some wine." He pats the tubes of belladonna root still hidden within his doublet.

Chad Michael Cox

"No." She pulls the ribbon from his hands. "I'll get the wine."

Maldinado watches her move through the masqueraders like a river flowing into the sea. Then she is gone. He starts toward the spot where she disappeared. Frantically searching. She emerges once more, holding two goblets above her head, trying not to spill as she makes her way toward him.

The crowds huddle and separate as the dancers prepare for the toast. Taggles assemble a stage in the middle of the courtyard for the Adow and her First Etabli. They are joined by Gan and Erisyte. A pause while the goblets are filled. Conversation. Laughter. Expectation! Gan motions for silence. Erisyte holds two goblets, one of which he hands to Gan.

There is a commotion in the north corner of the courtyard. Daden, honored warrior of Adarian, chosen for the Second Greeting, brings forth the Adow's golden goblet.

~

Hintor is drunk. He sits on a tree branch, one of many topis who have climbed the trees to gain a better view of the Adow. Daden holds the goblet high so all can see, and moves with measured step. When he reaches the stage, he bows, extending the wine to the Adow. She takes the offering and Daden retreats.

Gan speaks. "When I offered the first Toast of Sark, I gave a speech that was beautiful and lasted long into the evening. Now it seems I have grown dull, and my speeches are like breaths. I welcome you to Adarian, my Adow, as Sark once welcomed me—with a kiss and a toast!"

The crowd cheers. The Adow turns to her right and lightly kisses the bronze fashioned lips of the First Etabli.

God of Another World: The Adow

She raises her goblet and drinks every drop of the wine. Gan turns to Erisyte. They kiss and drink. Every topi who has found a partner follows suit.

"Are you going to kiss me?" Nataline stands beneath the tree.

Hintor follows the voice, finds his love holding two goblets of wine, and promptly falls out of the tree into unconsciousness.

~

Maldinado kisses the stranger. Her lips are stiff, quivering. Her body tightens as he moves his arm around her, pulling her closer. She relaxes. Her lips soften. They are the last to drink their wine.

Behind them, the tongued-one watches. He has watched them from the moment his daughter took the Madar's hand and began to dance. There are tears in Ayson's eyes as he watches. It's a moment of joy for his daughter, something he's never been able to provide.

The screams begin.

The Adow, Aiya *posing* as the Adow, has fallen to her knees. Faunride is crouched beside her, no longer wearing the mask of the First Etabli. Ayson runs after his daughter. She has left Maldinado. She's dashing toward the stage. Chaos! The Adowian Guard converge on the courtyard. Run! Push! Scream!

Faunride removes the mask Aiya is wearing, finds her face completely red, her eyes dilated. She struggles against him as though mad. Gan searches the crowd in desperation.

"The Red Death!" someone shouts.

"The Adow is dying!" another screams.

Gan raises his arms in an effort to quiet the crowd. "She's not the Adow!" he announces. "She is *not* the Adow!"

The Adow and Ayson reach the stage. Both remove their masks, and Gan points to them. "This is your Adow. Silence! *This* is your Adow!"

A hush fills the courtyard. Faunride steps away from Aiya as the Adow takes her handmaiden into her arms. No one says a word. Aiya dies. When it's over, the Adowian Guard encircle the stage. All the masqueraders leave the courtyard.

Maldinado looks into the eyes of the Adow, realizing she deceived him. He's lost his honor. He's kissed the Adow—only the First Etabli can kiss the Adow! He leaves the courtyard still wearing his mask.

THE ADOW

Aiya takes the silk-wrapped package from Erisyte. He stands before me, half-naked. His bronze torso—every muscle defined as though Beaug sculpted him from marble. If he didn't already belong to the Overseer….

"May the Sphere protect you." He says with a slight bow.

"And keep you in his light." I respond.

I watch him leave, his back and shoulders. If you had to break tradition, mother, why didn't you choose someone like him? I turn to find Aiya looking after him, as well. "Come, Aiya. He is nice to look at, but there is much to do before the Greeting Feast."

"Open the package, first." Ayson is sitting next to a three-pane window reading a series of letters he requested upon our arrival.

The room is suitable, though not my favorite in the castle. Decorated in heavy green velvet and gold-plated furniture, the well-lit space serves as a preparation room for the Greeting Feast. There is a bathing room attached, and several mirrors along the walls. Thankfully, Aiya had the mirrors covered. Better to judge my appearance after I've had a bath.

"What's in the package?" I move to the table where Aiya set it down.

"Aiya," Ayson extends a letter toward her. "You need to read this. It's from your distant grandmother."

I remove the white ribbon and unfold the blue silk to reveal a mask and a white gown. Nothing more. "What is it?"

Ayson is behind me. "A moment of freedom." He hands me a letter similar to the one Aiya is reading, but this one has the seal of the Adow—she who reigned during the time when Cintyge was First Etabli. Her seal was a crowned swallow.

The handwriting is faded but still legible:

> *Wear this mask to the Greeting Feast, my daughter. Be free of your title for one night. Experience life like never before, and return to the feast often. It is the greatest gift I can offer you, and to all of the Adow. May the Sphere be with us and keep us in his light.*

Ayson holds me with a gentleness as foreign as the mask on the table. "It should have been your mother giving you this gift, but it's no less significant. The Greeting Feast is a masquerade created as more than a celebration. Aiya and Faunride will take our places, tonight. Though I don't envy them." He looks back toward the handmaiden. "You'll be swarmed by everyone at the feast. It's a pitiful sight."

Troq never told me about this. Maybe he didn't know. A secret passed down by generations of Adow, now mine to experience. Entrusted to my keeping. I grab for the mask, hold it to my face—look through the eyes as though I've discovered a hidden passageway.

"Who else knows about this?" I lower the mask.

God of Another World: The Adow

"Only Gan." Ayson responds. "He is the keeper of the letters and the masks. From what I know of the tradition, I believe it was his idea."

I raise the mask. Sometimes I love being the Adow!

I hug him. A little weird, but I'm so excited I don't care. "Come, Aiya! We both have to get ready." I pull her from her letter toward the bathing room. She'll be wearing more than my gown, tonight. "You're about to become the Adow."

Three hours later, Aiya is standing in the corner of the courtyard, barely able to lift a goblet of wine for all the topis surrounding her, and I am standing beside Gan. Unannounced. Unknown. Free to dance! I don't have to wait long. A topi extends his hand, a warrior by the look of him. He's wearing a golden doublet and matching mask.

Let the masquerade begin.

I consume him. I want to devour him. I haven't been this close to a warrior since Troq died. Faunride refuses to touch me. Ayson can't. This one–Tasa Ro! Never let me go, stranger. I dig into his back, rest my head on his chest. Never let me go.

The music changes. "I'm yours to pursue, stranger."

Another partner. He's shorter than me, and he's crushing my hand. That's enough–I'm done dancing for the moment. I need wine and something to eat. I'm starving! I look for Ayson, or Faunride. Aiya. But I'm alone. There's no one to fetch me wine. For the first time in my life, I have to get my own wine!

I walk toward the nearest barrel, snag an empty goblet from a taggle's tray, and dip it into the dark red of Adarian wine. It runs down my hand, staining the sleeves of my white gown. I don't care. Let it be ruined! I drink the goblet empty and dip two more times before turning my attention to food. I gorge myself on cheese and apples. Sweet bread covered in frosting. Lamb. Goose. More wine. No one serves them to me. I have to get it all myself!

The stranger in the gold mask returns. Good. I want to dance. I press my body against his, twirl away, and return. We dance for what seems like forever. Then I leave him with another partner. I am his to pursue, not keep. I want to try belladonna root.

Another partner, this one is large. Not fat and not tall. Thick. Even for an Adarian. "Where do I get some belladonna root?" I whisper.

"Look for the mask of the Red Death." He holds me closer. "You'll need gold."

An Adow doesn't carry gold. "I don't…"

He holds a finger to my lips. It's as big as my arm. "Consider it a gift."

He drops a pouch of gold into my hand. Then he's gone. That was too easy. I search the crowd for my father. The tongued-one is standing next to Inindu-horse, but his attention is elsewhere. Is this part of the gift? Hard to say. Either way, I'm grateful…and thirsty. More wine.

The Mask of the Red Death greets me at the wine barrel. She wears a plain red mask, black robes. I exchange the gold for a tube of belladonna root, and she leaves—lost within the masquerade. I dispense the powder into my goblet and consume the drug.

Colors swirl. The masks grow larger, more ridiculous. I twirl in a maze of dance and laughter. Wow—I'm not even touching the ground! Every mask is more hilarious than the last. I move from partner to partner with a glee I can hardly contain. I can't feel my feet, or my face. I dance with everyone and no one. I'm struggling to focus on anything. Everything is a blur…

THE ADOW

I'm standing in the courtyard. No one is dancing. There are white ribbons. Everywhere white ribbons. The drug is wearing off. I'm not so dizzy. The stranger in the gold mask approaches, wraps me in a white ribbon. Yes, stranger. It's time to dance. Hold me steady.

I look into his eyes. Focus on his grey eyes…eyes like Maldinado's eyes. Maldinado! It is Maldinado! Dammit! Anyone but him. I pull the ribbon from his hands. "I'll get the wine." And run away…but I don't run away. This is my night. He'll never know it was me. Why shouldn't I kiss him?

He holds me in his arms, presses his lips against mine. This is my life. How it should have been before my mother ruined everything. Before Quel. I kiss him, linger on his lips, slowly pull away, and drink the last of my wine.

A scream rises. The masquerade comes to a sudden halt.

I am the Adow once more.

Chad Michael Cox

a taggle's tale

As spoken by a taggle girl who stood on the roof of Goleb's house in Adarian. Her tale began at sunset, two torches illuminated her face and movements, the emotion of both more pronounced by the flickering shadows upon her slender frame. Her voice was throaty, and her black hair blew freely. Only the bleating of a distant goat distracted the audience, but even that eventually faded. Her name was Dellina, and her mother had been my first love. She spoke in the manner of all taggles, for our story is a journey we share. May the Sphere forgive our mother and remember our father, as revealed in Dsal's vision.

- DK Vel

South of Adarian, just past the city walls, the taggle boy, DK Vel, follows his friend Beah down a hillside. The sky is overcast this morning and there is a mist in the air. Their torsos are slicked with moisture, their bare feet muddy and cold. DK Vel walks at an angle to keep from sliding down the hill. He feels the clumps of mud between his toes. He moves his hands from tree to tree, his fingers raw from grabbing at the bark, his knuckles red.

Forgive our mother
Remember our father

The boys head toward a community of taggles where Beah's uncle lives. The *dallic* is guarded by Adarian warriors who watch the boys as they reach the bottom of the hill, move past the stone wall, and walk the muddy streets. The images are familiar to the boys: a baby crawling in the mud, her mother nowhere to be found. Men gathered around a wagon, singing so low that their voices morph into a hum. The men are thin, worn, and scarred. A woman holds a baby to her breast, heads down the street. An ox follows her, every rib outlined by starvation. A taggle sits in the doorway of his hut. His face is painted red, and his eyes are closed in meditation. DK Vel recognizes him as the dallic *rivac*–chosen to pray to the Sphere…repeating the taggle's prayer over and over on behalf of the taggles living in the dallic. DK Vel and Beah bow as they pass the rivac. Then they utter the taggle's prayer.

Remember our father
Forgive our mother

The boys move through the dallic, encountering a taggle lying face down in the mud. He is bruised, beaten. He is dead. DK Vel imagines the moment right before his death. That is the moment when all taggles discover their destination, discover whether or not the Sphere listened to the taggle's prayer–remembered them or forgot about them. This taggle was forgotten, the boy decides. He imagines the fear in the man's eyes as he realized his fate…the sudden gasp for air before collapsing in death.

Beah leads DK Vel into a hut that has a hole in the wall just left of the entrance. It is dark inside, the only light streaming through the hole and slits in the roof, but it offers protection from the mist. Five taggle boys are huddled together inside the hut. They each have one hand extended with their fingers interlocked in a game that DK Vel does not recognize. He looks around. An older taggle sits smoking a pipe. Two women are asleep beside him, a third is speaking with three men—two of them much younger than the third who is growing a beard. Three girls are painting various designs on newly fashioned clay bowls, one of them smiles as DK Vel notices her. He finds himself staring at her as though he has never seen a girl before. Certainly, he has never *noticed* one before.

Beah addresses the taggle smoking a pipe. "Uncle, this is DK Vel. We have come for your blessing."

Beah's uncle puffs at his pipe, smoke lingering around his mouth. His beard is full and white, outlining his sallow cheeks. He is old, much older than any taggle in the dallic, a sign he has been blessed by the Sphere. "What dallic are you from?"

"Yenul."

"Is there no one to bless taggles in Yenul?"

"No one," DK Vel says.

Beah's uncle lowers his pipe. "You and Beah must earn my blessing."

"We are ready, uncle. What must we do?" Beah asks.

Beah's uncle looks the boys over from head to foot. "Ilion."

The young man with the growing beard steps forward. "Yes, Father?"

"Take them with you tonight."

Ilion nods and leaves with a promise to return. DK Vel doesn't notice. He is staring at the girl. She is staring back. A strand of hair covers part of her face. Her eyes are white—not yellow or bloodshot like the boy is used to seeing. Her skin is unblemished, as though never bruised or beaten. She is beautiful.

"Stay with us until Ilion returns," the old taggle says.

"I am honored, uncle," replies Beah with a bow.

DK Vel turns from the girl and bows. "I am honored."

They join the circle of boys sitting next to the entrance and, once the game is explained to them, they raise their hands, twist their fingers, and compete with the other boys. DK Vel, glancing at the girl painting the clay pot, finds she is still watching him. He returns his attention to the game, suddenly eager to win.

~

Several hours later, the taggles huddle together in sleep with Beah's uncle positioned in the middle of the circle of bodies and DK Vel, being the newest taggle to join the group, lying on the outermost perimeter of the circle. He can't sleep. By luck or coincidence, the girl is pressed against his chest, her position within the circle, one row deeper, aligning perfectly with the boy's own position. Her name is Della. He is holding her. He can feel her breath on his hand. Before DK Vel joined the circle, Della slept with her back exposed. Now her hair covers his face like his mother's used to when she would hold him close, keep him warm. She was the only woman he had slept beside, until now. He closes his eyes, buries his nose into Della's hair, and tries to fall asleep.

~

He is awakened by Beah's hand on his back. His friend motions for him to follow. It's still dark. DK Vel slowly removes his arm from around the girl, quietly rolling away from the circle of taggles. He follows Beah outside where they find Ilion crouching. The boys crouch beside him.

Chad Michael Cox

"Say nothing," Ilion whispers.

They follow him through the dallic, every step measured. When an Adarian guard comes into view, they fall to the ground and immediately roll through the mud into the shadows of a nearby hut. The guard passes and they are on the move once more. The air is cold, but DK Vel is sweating. Wherever Ilion is taking them, the boy understands the nature of their journey. If they are caught sneaking around at night they'll be killed.

Another guard comes near, but the taggles avoid being caught. When it's safe, Ilion moves. His pace quickens. It's darker in this part of the dallic. The growing smell of rotting flesh tells DK Vel they are headed toward the open gravesite where taggles are thrown when they die. Every dallic has one, and though they serve as the final destination of all taggles, they are rarely visited by those still living.

DK Vel and his friends descend into the mass grave.

"We're safe now," Ilion says. "The guards don't patrol the grave."

DK Vel can feel the ground shifting below his feet, the feel of cold flesh under his toes. He leans against the side of the pit in order to keep his balance as they walk, testing every step before moving forward. His imagination runs wild with images of bodies. They reach for him, their hands pulling at him. He breathes deeply to keep from panicking. Then he can hear Ilion rummaging–digging through the bodies, eventually opening a trap door that moans so much the boy is sure the guards will hear them.

"There's a ladder here. Be careful."

Ilion helps the boys find the ladder and DK Vel follows Beah down the opening. Above him, Ilion closes the entrance, another moan. The darkness is disorienting, the ladder his only sense of reality.

"There's a tunnel below," Ilion calls down to Beah.

"Where are we?" DK Vel asks.

"The dallic used to be a marble quarry. The workers used these tunnels until the marble was gone. Most of them have been destroyed or forgotten, but a few remain. This one was found by a taggle who hid among the dead. It saved his life."

"What's down here?" Beah asks.

"Your blessing."

Ilion leads them down the tunnel toward a glowing light. DK Vel tries to make out his surroundings, but it's too dark. He imagines the tunnel years ago, workers moving around, eating–their dread each morning as they faced the marble. He wonders if they ever saw Beaug, sculptor of Adarian, when he came to the quarry to select another block of marble. He wonders how many of them died in the quarry.

The glowing light is a torch. When they reach it, Ilion takes it in hand and leads the boys through the darkness. Soon, they are climbing over large stones and piles of rubble. DK Vel slams his toe into one of the stones. The pain is jarring. He bites his lip to keep from crying out. He continues gingerly, scrapes his calf and chest before Ilion can lead them back to solid footing. In the dim light, DK Vel can see a gash on Beah's arm.

Ilion talks while they walk. "You want to believe a taggle can be blessed, Beah–that there is more to this life. You want to believe my father can give you something the Adow denies you–but you're wrong. There is no blessing for a taggle! My father lives in the dallic same as the taggles who honor him." Ilion stops and turns toward the boys, his face a horror of shadow and light. "What blessing do you seek?"

"I wish to survive the Torment," Beah says.

"I want an Adowian Burial." DK Vel admits.

"Why do you wish to survive? Why do you seek an Adowian Burial? Because you're taggles, and taggles don't survive quests to the Torment. They don't receive Adowian Burials."

"I *will* survive!" Beah declares.

"You hope, yes. You pray for a miracle. But you will die. A blessing from my father won't change the fate of a taggle."

"Then why bring us down here?" DK Vel asks.

Ilion turns and begins moving once more. The boys follow until he stops and says, "Sanbi, it's me, Ilion."

He leads them into a small room where five women are waiting for them. They are all pregnant, except for one, who sits on the only blanket in the room. In her arms she holds a newborn child to her breast. The ears of the child are unaltered. Unscarred. Untouched by the blade of an Adarian guard. Ilion leans down and kisses both of them, then turns to the boys. "This is my cousin, Beah, and his friend DK Vel. They're here to help. Boys, this is Sanbi." He runs his hand over the head of the baby. "And this is Lay-I, her unmarked daughter."

"I don't understand," Beah says.

"Lay-I is your blessing. Deliver her to the Fire of the Sphere. The Daughters of Oblation will raise her as their own. She will be spared the life of a taggle."

"They'll kill us if we're caught." DK Vel says.

Beah protests, "You can't ask us to do this!"

"No. I can't ask you to do it. This is a choice *you* must

make. But you must decide quickly." Ilion takes Lay-I from her mother and holds her in his arms as though she were his daughter. Perhaps she is. "Many taggles pray and hope that the Sphere remembers them when they die, but when my father was still young, he decided he would give the Sphere a reason to remember him; something the Sphere could not ignore. He's saved dozens of taggles. Risked his life time and again, without a second thought, because he wanted to spare these babies the life we know. And the dallic has honored him. They know what he has done for their children. So here's your blessing, Beah. Deliver Lay-I and the Sphere will remember you when you die. It's the only blessing you'll receive."

"You're wrong," Beah says. "I'm in the Adowian Army. The Sphere remembers everyone who serves the Adow."

"You'll die a taggle," Ilion says. "Whether you die in the Torment or risk your life for Lay-I, you'll still die."

"I won't die tonight. Not like this." Beah says.

"Did you come to the dallic for a blessing, or to boast that you serve in the Adowian Army?" asks Ilion.

"Enough! I won't do it."

Sanbi is looking at DK Vel. "Will you save my daughter?" she asks.

The taggle boy stares at the baby. Her red hair scrambled about her head. Her tiny hand resting against Ilion's chest. "Yes. I'll take her to the Fire."

"May the Sphere forgive your mother," she says.

"And remember my father," DK Vel replies. "How do I get there?"

"This tunnel will take you under the walls of Adarian." Ilion says. "Once you're inside the city, you'll see the Fire."

Beah stares at his friend, aghast. "Why would you do

this? You won't make it. They'll catch you."

"They won't catch me." DK Vel turns to Ilion. "Show me the way."

~

"The night is no place for a taggle," Inindu says.

DK Vel freezes, slowly turns to find the magenta colored horse and rider. The creature is beautiful, more beautiful than the girl in the dallic. He tries to say something, but his lips won't move. Lay-I begins to cry, sensing the fear in her would-be savior.

topi-Inindu slides off Inindu-horse and takes the baby into her arms. "This is a yearling," Inindu says. "Explain yourself, taggle."

"I served her mother," the boy begins. "She died tonight, and there is no one else to look after her. I'm taking her to the Fire of the Sphere. Please, let me go."

Inindu holds the baby to her chest and begins to rub her back. "What is her name?"

"Lay-I."

She touches her nose with her own. The baby's crying ends with a giggle. Inindu does it again, remembering a time before Adarian's death. A time when Inindu, not a warrior, was the caretaker of the Daughters of the Adow. So much has changed. "I will take Lay-I to the Fire."

The taggle boy runs away without a backward glance, confirming what Inindu suspected. He was too eager to leave the baby. The boy was lying. "How did you escape the dallic?" She should follow him. Then again, the taggles are Gan's problem. Why should she care if they are sneaking around his city? She's never understood the Adow's curse upon the taggles, the forced mutilation of their ears. Inindu inspects the ears of the baby, once more, just to be sure. "An unmarked taggle…" The Adow would be furious. She smiles. "All the more reason." She looks up toward the Adarian castle where even now the Adow mourns the death of Aiya, completely unaware of the world around her. Typical! Inindu looks again at the baby. "All the more reason!"

Inindu takes Lay-I to the Fire of the Sphere, but she doesn't enter the sanctuary. She leaves the baby with a Daughter of Oblation, and promises to return…one day.

THE ADOW

When Troq died I ran and hid. I cried for days. Then Faunride assumed Troq's role as my protector and I attacked him. More than once I beat him with my fists because he wasn't Troq. Faunride would stand there until I pulled away, furious.

When my mother died I stared at her body, waiting for her eyes to open, her lips to move—waiting for her to tell me what I was supposed to do now that they had anointed me Adow. Her body emitted an odor, the smell of death; strange to be so repulsed by someone who looked so much like me—my reflection, her bloodless face withdrawing from the world. She was dead. I was transfixed upon her closed, translucent eyelids. Waiting for them to open.

Now Aiya is dead. I'm alive because of her, a strange comfort. Beyond comfort…grateful. She is the only one who has ever died to protect me. Grateful. Horrified. Sad. She's gone.

I turn over. Ayson is snoring—his bald head wrinkled, gathered against his green silk pillow. My champion sleeps.

Aiya is dead and Ayson is sleeping like nothing happened! I have the sudden urge to kick him out of bed. I get up instead, head to the door and open it. Faunride is standing guard. I knew it would be him.

"My Adow!" He bows.

I move into his arms. "Hold me."

For once, he does.

~

I'm awoken the next morning by Inindu pouring a pitcher of water on my head.

"Tasa Ro!" I'm soaked.

"That takes care of your bath. Now let's get you into some different clothes."

Inindu disappears into the next room. Ayson is still sleeping, slowly stirring awake. This time I do kick him. He sits up with a start, rubbing his face, trying to figure out what just happened. He looks at me with even more confusion.

Inindu emerges carrying a blue gown with silver inlay and a series of diamonds dangling from around the waist. She tosses the gown at me.

"Why are you here?" I ask.

"I heard you needed a handmaiden." There is a knock on the door. Inindu opens it and takes a serving tray, filled with apples, from a taggle boy. She closes the door and begins to eat.

Watching Inindu move about the room, watching her talk and gesture, both topi and horse, it's…too early in the morning for this! I'm soaked!

"Why are you wet?" Ayson finally notices.

Inindu lies down next to the door. "I gave her a bath."

I pull myself out of bed. My hair is sticking to my face. Water is dripping from my chin. "You're a horrible handmaiden."

"You're not much of an Adow." Inindu devours another apple.

"Who *are* you?" I suddenly realize how little I know about this magenta goddess. She was the first creature the Sphere created. She is eternal. Adarian dying...her tragic love affair. That's it. Troq didn't tell me anything about her, really. Certainly nothing about *this*! "You're this mythical creature that everyone feels sorry for, everyone pampers because you've lost your lover. That gives you the right to judge me? Aiya's dead! My mother is dead–in fact everyone is dead except him!" I point toward Ayson.

"That would solve a lot of problems, wouldn't it?" Something about her tone is frightening, as though plotting Ayson's death.

"She's the one who should have raised you." Ayson retrieves a knife from under his pillow, tosses it to the foot of the bed. "I'm yours to kill, Inindu."

"Why is that your answer to everything?" I yell at Ayson. It's way too early for this! Wait! "What does he mean you should have raised me?"

Inindu bites into another apple.

"She used to raise the Daughters of the Adow." Ayson climbs out of bed and walks to where his armor leans against the wall. He grabs his sword and flings it toward Inindu. "Maybe you'd prefer a sword?"

Tasa Ro! I drop the gown, pick up his sword, and heave it across the room. "You want someone to kill you then go find an assassin!"

"She *is* an assassin!" Ayson says.

"What?"

Inindu offers me an apple with a coy grin. "A taggle's story. Completely untrue."

God of Another World: The Adow

"Who are you?"

Inindu shrugs and bites into the last of the apples. I'm racing through every ounce of information Troq ever told me about her. He didn't tell me anything about her being an assassin!

Faunride cracks the door. "Is everything alright, First Etabli?"

"We're fine." Ayson says coolly.

Faunride hesitates, making eye contact with me before finally closing the door.

"I'm your eternal sister, my Adow." Inindu stands, horse and topi rising together, their combined presence a sudden force against which I find myself contending. She picks up the gown and holds it against my shoulder, intending for me to take it from her. "I trust you know how to dress yourself?"

Truth be told I've never dressed myself, but I'll be damned if I'm going to admit that to Inindu just now. I grab the gown and head into the bathing room, slamming the door behind me. What just happened? I collapse in a fury, strands of wet hair sliding slowly down my neck and cheeks. I turn the gown over in my hands. Where are the buttons?

~

An hour later, I'm sitting in front of my vanity while Inindu runs a brush through my hair as though she were hacking through a forest. "Ouch!"

"Every Adow has the same knotted hair."

"You don't have to be so rough. Ouch!"

"I stopped being gentle after the third Adow. It's better for both of us if I just rip through it."

"What was she like? The third Adow. Did you raise her?" She who reigned during the time when Aul was First

Etabli. I don't know anything about her. What were any of the Adow like? Did Inindu raise them all? Adarian's death must have driven her away from the Adow, leaving me with Troq and Faunride. Inindu stops brushing and I turn to face her before she can start again. I'm certain my head is bleeding.

Inindu looks into my eyes, a vacant stare as though seeking the remnants of the third Adow's spirit behind my own. Is she there? Do you see her? Ayson, sitting on the bed, in full armor, leans forward to hear Inindu's response.

"She loved to dance." Inindu turns me back around and cuts into my hair with the brush. "You remind me of her, the way you danced last night."

Last night…last night was incredible.

"I don't want to talk about last night. Ouch!"

"She was a quiet Adow. She kept her bedroom filled with Nelic Stems. They smell like smoke, but for whatever reason that was her favorite flower. She told me once their scent reminded her of our father…she was the last Adow to have ever seen the Sphere."

"She saw the Sphere?" I turn again. This time I take the brush from her. If she saw the Sphere she must have spoken with Him.

"She told me she did, and the two before her."

"Have you ever seen the Sphere? What does he look like?"

"Our father and I have never exactly…gotten along." Inindu takes the brush and begins anew. "Don't you keep a taggle around to tell her the ancient stories, Ayson?"

"Haven't you heard?" Ayson asks. "The Adow cursed the taggles. They get a little nervous whenever she's around."

"I didn't know taggles told stories." I've never even

God of Another World: The Adow

heard a taggle speak let alone tell a story.

Inindu turns me around—there's no more hair for her to yank out. "You're a poor excuse for an Adow."

"And you're no handmaiden." I run my fingers over my throbbing head.

Faunride enters the room with a bow. "The preparations are ready, First Etabli. Aiya's Final Cleansing will begin as soon as you arrive."

Aiya is dead.

I take and hide the brush in a vanity drawer. I look in the mirror. Aiya looked like me. My mother looked like me. They're both dead. I touch the blue velvet of my gown; trace the intricate embroidery around the neckline.

Faunride is watching me through the mirror. Our eyes meet for a moment before he turns away. That's the second time in one morning. The guard who insists upon formalities! *My* Faunride! And last night, he held me…

"So tell me, Ayson." Inindu exits the room ahead of us. "Have you ever died protecting your Adow?"

It strikes me she may be serious. Assassin or not, there is a lot to like about my sister, and a lot to learn.

Chad Michael Cox

a taggle's tale

As told by a taggle man who traveled with three warriors from Catareb. It is the first known instance of a taggle tale being told while in motion, without the benefit of a stage. The taggle's hands were tied, as is common these days. His breathing was heavy, the result of a previous day's beating, but he told his tale with every ounce of strength he had, and, by all accounts, as told by the taggles who traveled with him, these were the last words uttered by the man. His name was Phire. I met a boy named Phire in Lor, so eager was he to hear my tales he spent several months following me everywhere I went. This tale was one I told often in those days, leading me to believe the boy and the man were the same. He spoke in the manner of all taggles, for our story is a journey we share. May the Sphere forgive our mother and remember our father, as revealed in Dsal's vision.

- DK Vel

The inner city of Adarian, called Chance, is filled with single-level, square clay buildings. Door and window frames are all painted with vibrant colors like blue, red, yellow, or green. The rooftops of each building serve as marketplaces. Inside are taverns where games and lovemaking are a constant. Though many visit this part of Adarian, only a few actually inhabit it. The scholars have long believed the town to be ensnared in the struggle between the Sphere and Morlac; they say it's Morlac's only connection to the land. That is what the scholars say.

Maldinado knows it simply as home.

This is where his sister, Nataline, and her daughters live, the only home he cares to visit now that their father is dead. As for their mother, Breline–a Daughter of Oblation, she resides in the Fire of the Sphere. She made a vow, after their father's death, that she would never leave the four walls of the sanctuary. She never has, so Maldinado visits her when he comes home, but he makes his bed in his sister's home.

He sits on the edge of that bed, holding his head between his hands. He can hear Hintor and Nataline murmuring in the kitchen, the smell of sausage and breakfast rolls warming the morning air. The yearlings must still be asleep. They'll be up soon enough.

The Madar stands to look out the window. Mornings in Chance are quiet, but that will change. Aiya's final cleansing is today. After the ritual burning of her body at the Fire of the Sphere, the crowds will journey to Chance for a celebration. The Adow will come *here*. He touches his lips, scratches at his beard.

He kissed her.

A smile emerges between black whiskers. "Tasa Ro! I kissed her."

Maldinado watches two taggle boys move down the empty street. Chance used to be a collection of the dead and diseased–before Gan transformed the inner city. Now the bones of the dead serve as ornamental pieces. Bones everywhere. Skulls are used like vases, constantly filled with multi-colored flowers. Full-size skeletons stand guard at every door, dressed in bright colors and posed in very unnatural positions—most of them laughing. Bones. The colorful sculptures of Chance; such a contrast to the marble gray of the rest of Adarian.

"I kissed her!" Maldinado mutters.

~

DK Vel passes the home of Nataline with his friend Beah. He has never seen Chance. It is wonderful. The colors remind him of the beautiful creature who took Lay-I. *Inindu*. Beah told him the stories about Inindu when he returned to the dallic that night.

"Maybe seeing Inindu was my blessing." DK Vel says.

"Your blessing was you survived." Beah says. "I didn't think I'd ever see you again. I told Ilion as much, but he said you would return."

"I've never been so scared in my life."

~

The source of his fear, Inindu, enters the inner-city. Her lover, so often the subject of Beaug's work, does not adorn the sculptures of Chance. There is no sign of him. If Adarian is here, he is unknown, for the inner-city does not celebrate his life. They celebrate death, and the dead are unknown, unnamed. Nevertheless, there is always a celebration in Chance, which is why she has come. That, and she refuses to enter the Fire of the Sphere. The Adow and her First Etabli can tend to the burning ceremony. Inindu will not enter the Sphere's dwelling place.

She hears music and turns down a side street toward the sound of happiness. If Adarian is here, he will be where there is music and dancing. She holds her magenta hair to her nose. So long ago. His scent is all but gone. Once, it was strong, like lilac or warm honey. Now it's a peeled potato floating in cold broth. She misses him, but he will

God of Another World: The Adow

return to her one day. He promised to return.

She enters a large square. Inindu is not the only one skipping the burning ceremony. Hundreds of Adarians dance in a flurry of brightly colored gowns and instruments. The noise is pleasing and welcome. Inindu helped Gan transform Chance. She lived here during the Completion of the Red Moon, and for a time during the Changing of the Silver Moon. She walked these streets and danced here. It hasn't changed. The song is the same.

The music still consumes her.

~

In the same part of Chance, on the same street, an assassin enters a tavern. He orders beer and sits at a crowded table. The long table is laden with fruit, meat, bread, and cheese; and several of the most amazing breakfast rolls he has ever tasted. Streamers hang from the ceiling. Confetti litters the floor and is piled against the walls and bar. He takes a drink and waits for a Scarlet to approach him. When she does, he follows her upstairs.

The room is empty, save a single bed without sheet or pillow. The Scarlet is undressed before the assassin closes the door. Afterward, she leaves the room with a jingle of coins, leaving the assassin lying naked on the bed. He listens to her fondle his gold until it fades into the broader sounds of the tavern, the sound of merriment. So much laughter and chatter. He wonders what it would be like to live in Chance. Eventually, driven by his craving of more breakfast rolls, he gets dressed and heads downstairs.

~

Above the same tavern, Maldinado and Hintor referee a yearling's game of *Blind Goat*. Kaletine and Belur take turns wearing a blindfold. Hintor spins them around. Then they have to retrieve a blue ribbon from Maldinado and attempt to tie it around the goat's neck—all the while maintaining their balance. The game is a favorite of the Adarian 45th, though they have *altered* some of the rules for the sake of the yearlings. The warriors of the Adarian 45th don't use ribbons, they throw knives. Once the goat has been killed, it is cooked and served with a toast to the champion.

"I'm getting hungry." Hintor intones. "Perhaps I should go next?"

"Don't you dare kill, Silar." Belur scolds. "She's the only goat we have!"

Kaletine lifts her blindfold. "Uncle Hintor!" But Maldinado wraps her with the ribbon. "Your mother could fix a nice goat stew when she gets back." The Madar says.

Both yearlings burst into tears, horrified at the thought. Maldinado and Hintor do their best to consol them, they tell them it was just a joke, but it takes several minutes to calm them down. Afterward, they refuse to play the game.

DK Vel holds the goat, but since the game is over, the taggle boy is free to return to his perch atop the tavern where he and Beah watch the scene in the street below. He is immediately transfixed with fear and wonder. The creature, Inindu, is dancing.

The crowd surrounds her, but she does not see them. She is consumed by the music she once loved…before she loved Adarian. The topi is joined to the horse. She moves over and under and around the horse like rain falling upon a sculpture. She climbs onto the horse, lies upon its back, and moves up the neck, hair and mane blending as one. The topi wraps her arms around the horse's neck and swings down to the ground, falling like a banner lowered after battle. She falls to her knees and bows before the horse. Then she rolls and hugs the horse's leg. She rises and ducks and twirls and falls, but the horse does not move—

as though the topi were worshipping before her god.

DK Vel and Beah watch with wide-eyes as Inindu falls out of her white gown. She is oblivious, raising her arms and wrapping them around the horse. The boys lean forward with curiosity. She is completely naked! The street is alive with movement, a wave of dancing, jumping, and movement. Some of the dancers match the rhythms of the music, and some don't—but everyone moves.

And Inindu is naked!

She looks up toward the boys, making eye-contact with them if only for a second. Did she notice them staring? DK Vel quickly turns away in embarrassment. He taps Beah on the shoulder and motions for him to follow, but his friend doesn't leave. Beah is mesmerized by the scene in the courtyard. DK Vel finds himself peaking, and then he is staring, once more.

Behind the taggle, Kaletine and Belur, with their goat closely in tow, descend the stairs to the tavern below with their mother who has returned from her morning deliveries to the various taverns around Chance. Maldinado, no longer tasked with looking after the yearlings, scans the rooftops. Hintor searches the street

"This is where the Adow will come." Maldinado says. "If the assassin is still in the city, this is where he'll strike."

"He'll be too distracted by Inindu." Hintor points.

The assassin, however, is not watching Inindu. He is in the tavern below eating his fourth breakfast roll. He sits listening for the loud stirring in the crowd that will signal the Adow's arrival. His plan is simple: maneuver through the crowd until he is dancing alongside her–then he will kill the Adow.

He watches as two yearlings leave the tavern with their mother who is pulling a goat behind her. He orders another beer and sneaks one more breakfast roll. Two bites later, a cheer rises in the street. Morlac has blessed him. The time has come. He leaves the tavern and moves into the street.

Faunride walks ahead of the Adow and First Etabli, struggling to clear a path through the crowd.

"I never knew such a place existed." The Adow says.

"Adarian is full of secrets." Ayson responds. The First Etabli is nervous. Even with the Adowian Guard spread throughout the crowd; and with Faunride beside him... "This is a bad idea. We should head back to the palace."

"I agree, First Etabli." Faunride yells back.

Confetti covers the Adarian sky, thrown from every rooftop as the Adow moves through the street. Ribbons. Sweets. Beads. Skulls, perched on poles, bob above the crowd. Shouts and screams. Hundreds of Adarians.

The Adow begins to move in rhythm with the music and joy. "We can't leave, yet. Where's Inindu?"

"She'll be in the center of the square." Ayson says.

"Lead the way, Faunride!"

~

Maldinado curses, "Furmec Ro! He could be anywhere!"

"They could all be assassins." Hintor agrees. He points to the crowd now gathered around them on the rooftop. "We could be standing next to one."

Birate, toward whom Hintor points, is a hands-length away. The tiny warrior is dancing with a Scarlett, and rather engaged in the effort. "Well, maybe not him." Hintor says.

"Look, she's here." Maldinado watches the Adow enter the square. She's beautiful, even from this distance. His lips begin to tingle, recalling the taste of her kiss. "May the Sphere be with her."

"And keep her in His light." Hintor looks along the

God of Another World: The Adow

rooftop to where DK Vel and Beah sit watching Inindu. "Taggle! Two beers!"

DK Vel jumps at the command. He pulls Beah with him as they disappear into the tavern below. "I've never seen anything like that." Beah says.

"You'll never see it again if you don't pay attention." DK Vel responds. "The Adarians didn't bring us here to stare." He takes two beers from the bar counter where another thirty have been pre-poured, waiting for a taggle to deliver them. "She is beautiful, though."

"Taggle!" Another patron yells.

DK Vel hands the beers to Beah. "Take these, I'll get *him*."

~

The assassin moves closer to his target, nimbly maneuvering through the square, blending into the jostling crowd. His hand rests on the knife at his side.

~

Ayson holds the Adow against his chest, one arm around her waist. He shoves his way through the crowd, perhaps a bit more forceful than he should, but it's better than the alternative. Too many Adarians have tried to dance with her. They're drunk. They're risking their lives!

Faunride leads the way to Inindu. Then turns with embarrassment. Ayson, as well. A crowd of onlookers is gathered, some staring; some swaying. The assassin is staring.

The Adow grins. "You're a wonderful dancer, Inindu."

"How was the burning ceremony?" Inindu asks.

"The decorations were nice. Aiya would have been pleased."

"Do you plan on standing there all night, or are you going to dance?"

Chad Michael Cox

The Adow looks down at her blue gown, gathering it in her hands. "It's such a nice gown. I think I'll keep it on a bit longer." She grabs Inindu's white gown and tosses it toward her. "I trust you know how to dress yourself? I'll need you before dinner. Don't stay too long."

Inindu stops dancing.

"Ayson, I think we've stayed long enough." The Adow whirls and follows her First Etabli through the crowd.

Maldinado and Hintor watch from the rooftop.

Inindu lets the gown fall, and resumes her dancing.

The assassin follows the Adow. Unknown. Unseen.

a taggle's tale

As spoken by a taggle boy in the middle of a bloodgrass field north of Adarian. There was a great deal of wind, so the boy was forced to contend with the rustling bloodgrass, but he was the master of his voice. His booming, powerful telling was heard by the audience in a manner that kept their attention. They formed a circle around him, but rarely did he turn his back on any of them for he paced the entire radius. He was tall for his age, and his face was darkened by a spattering of hair not yet able to form whiskers. His name was Beah, my friend. He spoke in the manner of all taggles, for our story is a journey we share. May the Sphere forgive our mother and remember our father, as revealed in Dsal's vision.

- DK Vel

"She can't do this!" Hintor raises his arms in a helpless plea. "What about the yearlings?" He stands to pace the kitchen.

"She's the Adow. She can do whatever she wants." Nataline calmly sips a cup of ginger tea. "The yearlings will stay with my mother."

Maldinado, leaning against the doorframe with his arms folded, suddenly shakes his head. "No! I won't allow it."

"It isn't your decision to make, Maldinado. You've said yourself I'm the best cook in Adarian. Apparently the Adow agrees. Besides, we could use the money. You can't support us forever."

"He doesn't have to support you. I'll send you everything I have." Hintor returns to his chair at the table. Then he leans forward with an idea. "Marry me! We'll move to Plenrid and take over my father's farm."

Nataline puts her cup on the table. "Now is not the time to speak of marriage."

"I forbid it! I don't want you anywhere near Dragon's Torment." Maldinado says.

"Me too!" Hintor affirms.

"Forbid? Do you think I didn't forbid Kanbis from dying? Do you think Adarian wives don't forbid their husbands from going off to war? But do we say anything? We line the streets to say goodbye with a cheer. We hold our husbands as they die in our arms. We tell our yearlings it will be alright."

Nataline stands to retrieve the tea pot from the orange tinted clay oven, wipes the tears from her eyes. She looks around at the brass pots, wooden spoons, cast iron pans... the jars of various spices, bags of flour, sugar—her knives hanging from hooks on the wall. She'll have to pack all of it. The cutting board Kanbis made her for their first anniversary, ragged with splinters around the edges. Her tin measuring cups—dented and deformed. She could use a new set, but it would throw off her measures. The set of bowls Kanbis brought back from Yenul...she wipes her cheeks, settles her gaze once more upon the two warriors who have forbid her to cook for the Adow. *Forbid* her!

"I can't protect both you and the Adow!" Maldinado says.

God of Another World: The Adow

"You're afraid I won't come back? Do you think death is something you can forbid? Whether I'm here or there, you can't control my fate." Nataline replies.

"I'll protect her." Hintor says. "You worry about the Adow."

"You won't have to." Maldinado leaves the kitchen. He walks outside, past the laughing, hunchbacked skeleton, through the streets of Chance, and straight toward the castle of Adarian. *She can't do this!*

~

Faunride enters the room with a bow. Ayson is reading in one corner. Inindu and the Adow are near the bed. "First Etabli, the Madar of the Adarian 45th requests an audience with his Adow."

"Come for another kiss, no doubt." Inindu is fidgeting with the buttons at the back of the Adow's red gown.

"Let him in, Faunride." The Adow responds.

"My Adow." Faunride bows out of the room.

Ayson grabs his sword from the table and moves toward the door. A moment later Maldinado enters and kneels, his eyes finding the Adow, her back turned to him. The Madar's look does not go unnoticed by the First Etabli who stands over him. He could kill him for touching the Adow—for kissing her.

"You're interrupting my preparations, Madar." The Adow says without turning around.

Maldinado stands. "Forgive me, my Adow. It's about your cook. There's been a mistake."

Inindu starts combing the Adow's hair, but the Adow turns and grabs the brush. Inindu shrugs and moves to the window.

"I fired the cook, didn't I?" The Adow stares down at the floor, slowly moving the brush through her hair.

"Teyo has found a new one, my Adow." Ayson replies.

"She's my sister." Maldinado waits for the Adow to make eye contact, but she doesn't look at him. "She has two yearlings."

The Adow finally does meet his eyes, but there is no warmth in them. "Her family status is not my concern, Madar. Your sister has been chosen to serve me. There is nothing more to discuss."

"You can't…"

Ayson reaches for his sword. "You may leave now."

Maldinado stares at the Adow a moment longer. The Greeting Feast is a distant memory. The Toast of Sark—her kiss. They meant nothing to her. "My Adow." He bows and turns.

"There is another matter." The Adow waits for Maldinado to turn. "We leave for Dragon's Torment at dawn. Gather your warriors and report to Faunride. The Adarian 45th will serve as an extension of my Guard. If there are dangers in the Torment, you will be the first to die." Maldinado notes a softening in her gaze. "I believe that was your request, was it not?"

"The Adarian 45th is honored." Maldinado bows out of the room, closing the door behind him as he leaves.

"Nicely done." Inindu says. "You can put your sword away now, Ayson. Our Adow won't need your services. She has a new sword to play with."

~

DK Vel and Beah follow Maldinado, Hintor, Nataline, and her yearlings up the steps to the Fire of the Sphere. It is early morning. Wet streets reflect the flames from the large fire atop the sanctuary. The Fire of the Sphere. DK Vel wonders if Lay-I ever made it here.

Inside the Fire are two hallways that lead to a series of

rooms on either side of an inner sanctuary. Maldinado leads them to the left, where his mother resides along with the rest of the Daughters of Oblation—separated from the Sons of Oblation to the right. He reaches the iron-gate, and speaks to the Daughter who approaches.

"We're here to see Breline. I'm her son."

"One moment."

The Daughter of Oblation turns and disappears around the curved hallway. DK Vel looks up at the towering ceiling; painted panels depicting scenes of creation, battle, and death. Most of them are of the Adow or the First Etabli, but some of the scenes are from the painter's imagination. Torches line the hallway, casting shifting light and shadow upon each panel, providing the illusion of movement within each painted scene. One of the scenes is a depiction of Adarian's death at the Battle of Ire. The Adow is holding his body, as is the traditional representation, but in the smoke behind them DK Vel notices a dark pink image the painter has all but concealed in the chaos of battle. There is no mistaking that image, concealed in the shadows the same as when the boy first met her in the streets of Adarian. When she took Lay-I from him.

The iron-gate opens and Breline emerges wearing a white robe and gold sash. In her arms is a bundle of blankets wrapped around a baby. Kaletine and Belur run to greet their grandmother, and the baby. Breline squats down so the yearlings can get a better look. "The Father of Oblation gave her to me; I suppose that makes her your aunt."

DK Vel can't take his eyes off the baby. *She made it!* He elbows Beah who has already made the connection.

Maldinado and Nataline stand at a distance, delaying their goodbyes, knowing their mother will cry. Breline looks up at them both with a look of resigned disapproval. Then she turns to Hintor. "I suppose you intend to leave me, as well?"

Hintor nods. "Someone has to look after these two."

Breline passes Lay-I off to Kaletine. "Gentle. Hold her head like this." She guides the yearling's arms until she is satisfied with the resulting cradle. Then she walks over to Hintor and gives him a hug.

"May the Sphere protect you, Hintor."

"And keep you in His light."

She wipes the tears already streaming down her cheeks, and turns to Nataline. "It isn't enough I give my son to the Adow—now she takes my daughter, as well?"

Nataline falls into her mother's arms. There are no words exchanged, their combined tears communicating everything they have to say to one another. Finally, Breline lifts her daughter's chin, gives her a kiss on the forehead.

Then Belur is hugging her mommy's leg. Nataline picks up her daughter and joins Kaletine who is still holding Lay-I. Nataline embraces both of her daughters even as Breline embraces her son.

"Protect her." Breline whispers.

Maldinado holds her head against his chest, kisses her hair. "I will."

God of Another World: The Adow

Dsal Tiger

This tale originated in the Adarian dallic, a warning to those who would seek comfort rather than devote their lives to the Sphere. The figure of Dsal Tiger has a short tail, according to Adarian tradition. His fur is orange except for the white around three of his paws, and he has black stripes. This tale was first told during the Great Snow. Many taggles died in those days.

I first heard this tale from Beah's uncle. The tale begins: Listen to these warnings, and may Dsal guide you to the Sphere.

- DK Vel

Dsal Tiger walks the streets of Adarian. It's snowing. He's cold. On his back is a layer of snow. He searches for fire that he might warm his paws and thaw out his whiskers, but the streets are empty. There is no fire. Only statues.

Dsal Tiger stops at a marble tree. "Do you have any fire?" he asks.

The marble tree shakes its limbs, sending a torrent of snow downward. "I don't have fire. My wood doesn't burn."

Dsal Tiger paws at the tree. It's cold. Lifeless. He lowers his head and leaves the marble tree. No one else moves through the streets of Adarian. His own path is hidden, his footprints quickly concealed by the falling snow. He wanders from one side of the street to the other, never walking in a straight line for the snow is blinding.

Dsal Tiger finds a marble river. "Do you have any fire?"

"I do not have fire," the marble river says, "for we parted long ago and have gone our separate ways."

Dsal Tiger again lowers his head in sadness. He tests the waters, but the surface is frozen over. His paws are numb. He is losing strength. He leaves the river, walks down another snow-covered street.

There, in the distance, he sees a marble flame. He manages to navigate the snow. Forces every step until he is beneath the fire. "Do you have any fire?"

The marble flame wavers in the howling wind. "I am the flame that burns forever. I am fire."

Dsal Tiger circles the flame, searching for the perfect spot to lie down, eventually curling up at the base of the statue. The marble flame offers no warmth. It is cold. But Dsal Tiger doesn't move. He has found his fire.

He closes his eyes, falls asleep, and slowly freezes to death.

DRAGON'S TORMENT

a taggle's tale

As spoken by a taggle boy at dusk in Dragon's Torment. He climbed onto a boulder and stood high above all the taggles who gathered to hear his tale. As they gazed up toward him, they marveled at how clear the night sky was and how many stars they could see. The taggle boy paused before beginning his tale, outlined by the stars. In contrast to his red hair, which glimmered at the edges, his face was in darkness. Yes, his whole body was a shadow against the sky. Thus he allowed the wonder of the moment to transform into horror, quite effectively enhancing his tale before he ever spoke a word. His name was Edran, Hiate's apprentice. He spoke in the manner of all taggles, for our story is a journey we share. May the Sphere forgive our mother and remember our father, as revealed in Dsal's vision.

- DK Vel

Caduum serves as the entrance to Dragon's Torment. It began as a trading post for the Rorne tribes, but the Rorne have not journeyed to Caduum since the Completion of the Yellow Moon. The buildings, neglected and battered by the winds that come from the Torment, have begun to bend, break, and crumble. Some of the buildings have collapsed completely. Rubble in the wind. No one cares. No one cares because no one travels to Caduum, anymore. Only those who were born here remain in the town, and they don't dare walk the streets. Instead, they reinforce their walls. They hide behind locked doors. They stare out their windows at the ghost-like images that haunt this dying town.

Hiate the blacksmith stares at an approaching figure. His apprentice, Edran, shakes with fear.

"'Tis the wraith of yer father come to fetch you, boy," Hiate teases. He looks at his apprentice who is standing slightly in front of him, holding a mostly-fashioned sword with both hands. "Wraiths won't be bothered with weapons. Yer sword be more useful on an anvil this night." The blacksmith looks down the street. The wind sends dirt and brush swirling through the air; imaginary figures and shadows in the night—then there is nothing. "He's left us, yearling. Come–back to the forge. We have swords to fashion for the Adow and her Army."

Still, the red-bearded blacksmith looks out into the street and almost whispers, "And pray yer father has forgotten about you."

~

On the other side of Caduum an assassin appears. He wears a red cloak, a leather strap securing the raised hood just below his nose; even so, dust penetrates the makeshift shield. Coats his mouth. He grinds the particles as he clenches his teeth and grimaces against the rage of wind from Dragon's Torment. He holds his arm around his eyes to shield them. He can't see and curses Morlac for sending him to such a place. The flicker of a candle appears, dulled by a window pane. The assassin dismounts and leads his horse toward the light. The light vanishes.

Another light. He walks toward it until he is looking through a six-pane window. The hood of his cloak gathers against the glass, forming a barrier from the wind, providing his bloodshot eyes some welcome relief. He can hear his breathing as he searches for signs of life. Someone appears from another room. She's wearing a white gown, her black hair hanging loosely about her shoulders. In her hand she holds a silver brush with black bristles. When she reaches for the candle, the assassin sees a small, milky-white birthmark on her forearm. Then their eyes meet.

She doesn't scream. She stares at him as though he were nothing more than a vague memory. The assassin leaves the window in search of a door, but he finds the wooden door reinforced by iron, made to stand against the winds of the Torment. He knocks, but his pounding is useless; a whisper in the storm. He returns to the window only to find darkness.

He turns and leads his horse down the street once more. The assassin hears the sound of splitting wood followed by the cackle of a shattering building. He flinches, moves away from the sound. The horse yanks against the reins and runs off.

"Tasa Ro!" He rubs at his hand.

Another light flickers. Staring out from behind a window is an old topi. His white hair is cut short and erratic. His throat is the size of his nose. His eyes look past the assassin into the streets of Caduum beyond. The assassin waves, hoping to get his attention, but the old topi doesn't notice. Doesn't even turn his head. The assassin follows his gaze into the street. Nothing there. He looks back at the old topi, still staring. The assassin motions once more, but there is no change in the topi's demeanor.

The assassin leaves him to his visions. There is no more

light. No signs of life. The wind swirls around him and Caduum all but disappears in a storm of dust. He is disoriented. He begins to count his steps, if only to assure himself he is moving. At thirty-two steps he is forced to walk around the remains of a wooden cart. At forty-three steps he finds the head of a donkey–the rest of its body buried by the dust. One hundred seventy-one. He finds an empty tavern. The roof of the building has collapsed and the door swings in the storm. Three hundred six. He bangs at the window of another home, candlelight barely aglow, melted wax pools around the flame. No one is visible in the darkness beyond the fading light.

More homes, a carpenter's shop, a stable, an inn, a trading post—all destroyed by the wind. Then he sees the glow of a forge; hears the pinging of a blacksmith's sledge. The workshop is undaunted by the wind, made from stone piled atop stone and reinforced by wide strips of wrought iron. There are holes for windows high upon the walls, but no glass. The wind flows freely through multiple openings, providing ventilation for the forge. There is an entrance, but no door.

The assassin enters and stands just inside the shop. The blacksmith is drawing out the rough shape of a sword, lengthening the metal with the peen of his hammer, raising and lowering the hammer in smooth, even strokes. The blacksmith has a beard and his thick red hair is pulled tight behind him. His muscular frame carries the weight of his extended—and expanded— waist. A taggle boy with matching red hair is kneeling behind him, taking inventory of a pile of already-completed swords.

"Eighteen," the boy says, looking up.

Hiate doesn't stop hammering. "Fetch me more Dragon's Ore." The taggle leaves just as Hiate notices the assassin. "You'll not find what yer seeking here, demon. The Torment be the only comfort for you." Hiate continues to hammer; keeping one eye on the assassin.

"There is nowhere else to go," the assassin says. "I've searched the town. No one would open their door."

Hiate stops hammering. "There's no door fashioned that keeps the wraiths away. You be no demon."

"I'm not a wraith, either." The assassin removes the strap from around his cowl, allowing it to fall. There is a mask of dirt around his eyes.

The blacksmith measures the assassin. "Have you a scar?"

The assassin smiles, "Is that how you greet everyone?"

Hiate sets the hammer on the anvil and pulls up his left sleeve to reveal a scar that wraps around his forearm near the elbow. "'Tis the only way to prove yer still alive in Caduum. When the wraiths appear, they be missing their former scars."

The assassin reveals a scar on his right leg. "I got this in a Catareb tavern. I was young and mostly drunk."

The taggle boy appears from a back room, carrying an armload of Dragon's Ore. His red hair hangs loose and gathers at his shoulders. When he sees the assassin, he drops the ore, picks up a sword, and charges. The assassin unsheathes his own sword, but Hiate moves to block the taggle's path.

"Calm yerself, Edran." Hiate reaches out and pulls the sword from the taggle's hand. "'Tis flesh and blood before you."

Edran stops. "Have you a scar?"

Hiate pats the boy on the head. "We've already discussed such matters, boy. Go, fetch broth and beer. 'Tis a more pleasant way to spend the evening than swordplay."

Chad Michael Cox

Edran leaves and the assassin sheathes his sword. "Where I come from, taggles are killed for such an attack."

"No doubt we'll all die soon enough. Come, sit." Hiate points to a row of metal chairs extending from the stone wall. "Tell me what you saw in the streets just now."

"Nothing," the assassin says. "There is nothing out there."

Hiate smiles, "Stay for a few more nights and you'll be seeing wraiths. My own father visits every third morning just before the sun arrives."

The assassin removes his cloak and sets it on the metal chair. He is warm from the heat of the forge. A lather of sweat coats his throat. "Why does he visit?"

Hiate laughs. "'Tis a question to be asked for certain, but it be one I've not thought to ask." He points to an iron chest on the ground behind him. "He comes through the doorway and walks to that chest. Then he disappears. Never says anything; never even looks around."

"What's in the chest?" The assassin asks a little too eagerly.

"Nothing." Hiate looks back toward the assassin with a suspicious stare. "I never understood my father when he be alive. 'Tis the same in his death. I used to avoid him, but now he's a welcome part of my morning, same as Edran fetching the ore."

The assassin continues to stare at the small, blackened chest. It is severely damaged, dented and rusted. There is no lock.

Edran appears, carrying a wooden tray with bowls of broth, three goblets, and a pitcher of beer. The taggle sets the tray down and hands the assassin his portion.

Hiate notices the confusion on the assassin's face as he lifts the bowl and goblet. "Broth first then the beer–like this," the blacksmith raises the bowl to his lips and proceeds to drink. A stream of broth runs over the edge of the bowl and down his chin. When the broth is consumed, Hiate raises the beer in a toast. "May the Sphere protect you." Then he guzzles it down.

"And keep you in His light." The assassin raises the bowl and feels the warmth of the broth move down his throat, followed by the rawness of the beer.

Edran joins the toast. "May the Sphere protect you." He drinks the broth, but when he reaches for the beer he finds it missing.

"And keep you in His light," Hiate says. He gulps down the beer and laughs at the apprentice. Edran gives him a look of irritation, places the empty goblets and bowls back on the tray, and sulks away.

As the night winds encircle the apprentice, the assassin sees a new figure appear—if only for a moment. He searches the night, but it's gone. "Did you see that?"

Hiate looks at the assassin. "'Tis a wraith you've seen?"

"It looked like my father."

"Didn't I tell you? Stay in Caduum and you'll see yer father, yer mother, and the Sphere himself. 'Tis what I said, yes?"

The assassin walks over to the doorway. He looks into the night winds. "How did your father die, Hiate?"

"'Tis a mystery." Hiate points toward the forge. "I found what was left of his body in the forge. My father was a…"

Hiate continues with his story, but the assassin only half hears him. He searches for the wraith of his father, struggling to see anything in the street. The assassin nods as Hiate nears the end of his tale. "So did he ever leave Caduum?"

A look of longing passes over Hiate's face. "No, a

smithy be cursed in that regard. Only our work travels the land. We have too much be needing our attention at the forge." Hiate turns back to his hammer. "Which serves to remind me the Adow's army is quickly approaching while I be raising and lowering my jaw instead of my sledge. There be a bed in my home for you. I won't be needing it, tonight. We all serve the Adow in some fashion, don't we?"

The assassin smiles as he retrieves his red cloak. "Yes, we all have our duties."

Edran returns to take the assassin to his room. A moment later, the assassin is sitting on the bed, listening to the muted sounds of the forge and hammer. He rubs at his stomach. The broth and beer slosh around, a warning of the nausea to come. Again, he curses Morlac for sending him to such a place; for sending him here to wait for the Adow.

THE ADOW

The wind is unbearable, but the sight of Caduum is welcome. After so many weeks with nothing but open fields of bloodgrass, it's nice to see some form of civilization. Perhaps the last we will encounter. Dragon's Torment looms large behind the town, every peak a barrier—a warning. The town is all but forgotten, and yet we've come. Thousands of warriors. I've led them here under the guise of a quest, the promise of a reward.

It's just a story.

Maldinado appears behind us, the wind dampening the sound of his horse. He hasn't stopped moving since we left Adarian, and I find myself watching his coming and going with great interest. No one has ever invested so much energy into my well-being. Not even Troq. His warriors are everywhere: scouting, guarding, reporting. He is constantly giving them direction, communicating with them. If Ayson was half the guardian Maldinado has been I wouldn't have so many scars. He reigns-in beside Inindu. His black hair whipping across his face. His eyes. I feel myself staring into his grey eyes…and he is staring back.

His attention turns to Inindu. "Have you ever been to Caduum?"

"Not since it was abandoned. It was built as a base camp with an intentional lack of hospitality. No one lives there now except ghosts."

"My scouts haven't reported back. Something isn't right." Maldinado leans forward in the saddle. Our eyes meet, though his comment is directed toward Ayson. "First Etabli, it may be wise to make camp here until they return."

"I disagree." Faunride responds tartly. He has been noticeably irritable since I recruited Maldinado to lead us into the Torment. "My Adow…" That's another thing! He's been addressing me directly ever since we left Adarian. "Despite its lack of inhabitants, my reports suggest there is shelter in Caduum. Something we could all use before we enter the Torment."

"I would avoid seeking shelter in Caduum." Inindu says. "It's as likely to cave in on you as protect you against these winds."

"I've heard similar stories, my Adow." Hintor says. He and Nataline, my new wonderful, exceptional cook, have been inseparable. I find them strangely comforting. "My father came here to trade a time or two when I was a yearling. He said the town was falling down around him."

"It sounds as though there is nothing left of Caduum." I respond.

"Teyo was there!" Faunride continues. "He commissioned several weapons from a blacksmith who lives in the town, and stated there were numerous buildings still erect."

"A blacksmith?" Inindu wonders aloud.

God of Another World: The Adow

THE ADOW

"Forgive me, First Etabli." Maldinado is still looking at me. "Faunride's information is over two weeks old. I'm not comfortable moving into Caduum until my scouts have had a chance to return."

"Can we go around it?" Hintor asks.

Inindu shakes her head. "No, Caduum serves as the only entrance to the Torment. A broken gate, but a gateway all the same."

"Have you ever been to the Torment?" Ayson asks…a bit off topic. "What's it like?" He's been distracted for the past few days, ever since Dragon's Torment appeared on the horizon.

Then again, I've been just as distracted.

"A veiled question if I've ever heard one." Inindu brushes her magenta hair away from her face. Not a single tangle! The wind moves her hair as though folding a napkin. It ravages through *my* hair! I swear I'm carrying a haystack above me. "The answer to your question is yes, Ayson, you will die in the Torment. Only a few are strong enough to survive."

I doubt if anyone will survive. Except Inindu. She's been there before. Maybe several times.

"Are the stories true?" Nataline asks with trepidation.

"Ask your taggle." Inindu points to a boy walking behind us, along with a dozen other taggles.

"Not now." Ayson gathers himself. "Thank you for your concerns, Madar, but Faunride is right. We are better served by the shelter in Caduum." Then he adds, "As for the stories…may the Sphere protect us."

"And keep us in His light." Nataline finishes.

"I have never known my father to protect anyone in the Torment." Inindu says.

"The Sphere is everywhere!" I don't even know why I

said that. How do I know? He doesn't speak to me.

"Have you heard the story of Dragon's Torment?" Inindu chides.

Of course I...*haven't*. Tasa Ro! "Which story?" Surely there are several stories. Hopefully? Please don't tell me it's the story about the five wolves. Does she know about Troq's story? The five wolves? Yes, Inindu–this quest is nothing but a story Troq used to tell me! I lied!

"The origin of Dragon's Torment."

She doesn't know! "Yes, I've heard the tale–or at least part of the tale. The Sphere created the Torment to serve as a prison for Morlac."

"The god of another world is not so easily contained." Inindu warns. "It was not my father who created the Torment. It was Morlac. The Torment is not a prison. It's a barrier meant to keep the Sphere from entering."

"Blasphemy!" Faunride accuses. "May the Sphere protect us."

"And keep us in His light." Inindu responds, sourly, taking Faunride aback. Again I'm left to wonder how much I really know about Inindu.

"Why would Morlac want to imprison himself?" Hintor asks.

Inindu flashes a wicked smile. "Perhaps we are the ones imprisoned, and Morlac has managed to escape."

I stare at the outline of peaks across the horizon. Dragon's Torment. Forbidden. Troq warned me–the tiger died at the end of his story! Now I've led my entire army to Morlac's doorstep. No, this isn't us on the verge of escape. We aren't prisoners. We're fools who are about to die.

I sneak a peek at Maldinado. He isn't looking at me. Neither is Faunride. To my surprise, Ayson is the only one paying me any attention. He takes my hand in his–squeezes

THE ADOW

it as if to assure me everything will be alright.

But that's *not* how this story will end!

~

Two hours later, I enter the home of an old topi who cowers in the corner of a hallway. Teyo is talking to him, trying to calm him down.

"It's no use." Hintor says. "Look at his eyes. He's mad. Probably doesn't even know we're here."

"How could anyone live in such a place?" Nataline wonders as she moves to the kitchen.

The old topi is shaking his head from side to side muttering, "'Tis a wraith, 'tis a wraith, 'tis a wraith…" His eyes are clouded over, as white as his beard. His skin is translucent with age, falling from his bones as though mimicking the white gown that is pulled over his knees and left to scatter over the wooden floor at his feet.

Perhaps we *are* the ones imprisoned.

I leave the hallway and enter a large room filled with cobwebs and dust. Oversized chairs are covered in a rough canvas looking material. The walls are cream with a stone fireplace opposite the doorway. There is a dark-stained wooden bookshelf surrounding the fireplace, barren except for three books stacked on top of one another. The only window in the room faces the street outside where I can see Inindu, a magenta blur through the white film of the glass. She refused to enter a building she said would collapse before nightfall. I'm a little uneasy, myself.

Maldinado quickly conducts a search for would-be assassins. "Have your scouts returned?" Ayson asks.

"No." Maldinado looks up the chimney, jabbing his sword into the darkness. "I've sent out a search party. We'll find them or we'll find the reason they're missing." He turns from the chimney to look at me. "It's safe, my

Adow."

Safe. Yes, I have never felt safer.

Or more exposed.

We will enter Dragon's Torment tomorrow. Everyone will die. My beautiful Maldinado. I could save him with a single command. I could tell him this is all a lie. But the devastation he'd feel would be far worse a death. Not just Maldinado. They all believe in me. They willingly give their lives for me. To take that away from them…

"Thank you, Maldinado." I respond.

There is nothing more to say. My thoughts drift to my mother. I wonder if this is how she felt when she led her army into Quel. How many died for her because she selfishly chose Ayson over Yenen?

Our story is the same! Despite everything!

I grab my father's hand. I don't know why…because he's the only one I *can* grab! I can't touch Maldinado. Faunride is off seeing to the army. Who else is there? My mother used to hold his hand. I always thought it was a show of affection. Now… I wonder is she held him out of desperation, an awareness of who she was–who I've become.

I drag Ayson back into the hallway, away from the old topi still muttering craziness, and cautiously climb a staircase. The stairs creak with age, for the planks are dry and several of them are split. I half expect to fall through at any moment, ending this whole charade, but we manage to reach the top without incident. There are two rooms, but I'm not in the mood to explore. Ayson follows me into the room nearest the staircase, and I close the door, leaning against it with my back.

I'm still holding his hand. This is my father, his bald head oddly visible in the darkness, catching the glow of light from around the door.

"What's wrong, my Adow?"

I move into his arms and rest my head against his course tunic. "Nothing."

He kisses the top of my head.

No, something is wrong. Everything about this quest is wrong! "They'll all die because of me." I mumble.

"No." He pulls my chin up so I'm looking straight at his darkened face. "They'll die because you gave them a reason to die."

I pull away from him and find my way to the shadowed outline of a bed. It feels good to sit on something other than a horse, though it doesn't offer much padding, and I can smell the dust now swirling around me. When was the last time someone slept in this bed? How long has that topi been sitting in the hallway downstairs?

I lean forward into my hands, letting my eyes fully adjust. The room looks to be mostly undecorated, only the bed and a small table. How did I ever wind up in this place? Worse yet, an entire army followed me here. Yes, I've given them a reason to die, but it's all a lie.

I turn back toward my First Etabli, a figure of shadow now framed by light visible through cracks around the door. "Is that what you told my mother before Quel? She gave them a *reason* to die."

"That's what she told *me*." Ayson moves to sit beside me on the bed, resulting in another unseen dust cloud. "I was convinced that I was the reason so many warriors died at Quel. I could see it in the eyes of every warrior who followed your mother into battle. They may have fought against Yenen, but only because they fought on the side of their Adow. I knew what they thought…what they still think about me. I knew they were going to die because of me, but your mother…"

"She never did care what anyone else thought." I finish his thought. There's a reason no one liked her.

"She cared–she cared more than you can imagine. No, I was going to say your mother wouldn't let me feel sorry for myself. She told me I wasn't the reason they were dying. I was simply giving them a reason *to* die. In a way, I brought honor to their death."

Ayson puts his arm around me. "The truth is a warrior doesn't want to die of old age. Look at me–I'm weak. I'm not the warrior I used to be. I find myself leaning more and more upon Faunride, these days."

The smell of dust fades, replaced by the bitter scent of my father, a mix of cooling sweat and chainmail.

"I've been thinking a lot about this quest." He continues. "I'm ready to die. In fact, I want to die! If only to bring honor to you and your mother. Even if I have none."

He lifts my chin, again. "And when I die promise me you'll make Faunride your First Etabli. I've seen the way you look at Maldinado. It's the same way your mother used to look at me, so I know you love him, but it doesn't matter! Don't make the same mistake! Faunride should be the next First Etabli…just like your mother should have chosen Yenen over me. I realize that now. It was all wrong."

It's true, I do love Maldinado, but the Madar will die alongside everyone else. "Alright." I nod. Faunride will be my First Etabli. Faunride, my ever-prudish guardian… imagine his face when he finally, willingly, sees me naked.

Ayson pulls me closer, resting his chin upon my head. "Anyway, your mother was right, but she was also wrong. I wasn't the one who gave them a reason to die. No one is willing to die for a First Etabli, especially one they don't believe in. But it doesn't really matter who serves as First

THE ADOW

Etabli—even Adarian never inspired his warriors to die for his sake. No, the Adow is the reason they follow. They will always follow their Adow. You are the reason they live and the reason they die. If all of those warriors die tomorrow they'll have died willingly, and because of that they will die with honor."

I have no response, and I'm tired of discussing it, anyway. I just let him hold me. Truth or lies, it all leads to the same death.

I am their Adow. This is my inescapable prison.

a taggle's tale

As spoken by an old taggle woman to a group of customers gathered around her fruit cart in the Yenul marketplace. The geyser above the cavern roared in the background, a constant presence she used to simulate the winds of Caduum. She was a hunchback. In general an ugly woman, but her looks accentuated her gestures and she was full of energy. At one point, she hurled her fruit into the crowd, at another point she pulled at her hair. She danced and twirled around her wooden cart to such great effect that she transported her audience from Yenul into the hell of Caduum. Her name was Janeel. She did not journey to Dragon's Torment with us, probably had never seen Caduum, but she had gathered enough details from those who purchased her merchandise over the years to complete her tale, and it is consistent with what I remember. She spoke in the manner of all taggles, for our story is a journey we share. May the Sphere forgive our mother and remember our father, as revealed in Dsal's vision.

- DK Vel

The assassin moves through the streets of Caduum. He has already killed two Adarian scouts, but they were not his target—merely a necessity. He would have preferred not to kill them, after all he left the blacksmith and his apprentice alive, but there was no other option. He needed their armor. It's the only way he'll get close enough to the Adow.

In the chaos that is Caduum, he moves freely through wind and dust. The Adowian Army doesn't even notice. They are busy constructing shelter, or they huddle together inside mostly damaged buildings. The few who do notice him think nothing of it because there are many warriors moving around in the night, and why should they worry about such things?

The assassin searches the scattered encampment for the banner of the Adow. It doesn't take long. The fools have it waving outside the building where she is staying, announcing her presence, all but inviting him to enter. But he doesn't need an invitation. He merges with the Adarian warriors who surround the structure, his unfamiliar features hidden by the swirling dust.

Maldinado, unaware of the assassin's presence, sits in the kitchen with Hintor and Nataline. "There's one good thing about you serving the Adow." He says to Nataline. "I don't have to worry about her food being poisoned."

"We don't have to worry about going hungry, either." Hintor lifts a spoonful of warm butternut squash.

Faunride enters the kitchen with two empty plates. "The Adow and First Etabli pass along their compliments and a request for seconds."

"Of course." Nataline replenishes the plates with generous helpings of squash, chicken, brown rice, and ginger pudding. "Shall I make another plate for you?"

"No thank you. I'll eat once the Adow has gone to bed." He casts a glance at Maldinado who is chewing a mouthful of rice. Then he leaves, returning to his post outside the Adow's bedroom.

"Well that was odd." Hintor says.

Chad Michael Cox

"He's been giving me those looks since we left Adarian."

Nataline sits down at the battered wooden table. "You've been giving him the same looks. The two of you could be less obvious, you know."

"Not to mention the way you and the Adow cast eyes at each other. It's nauseating." Hintor scrapes his plate.

"You should talk." Maldinado counters.

Hintor looks up from his plate then points with his spoon toward Nataline. "We're practically married."

Nataline takes the spoon out of his hand. "We're not married, yet." She says. Hintor smiles awkwardly around a mouthful of food while Nataline replenishes his plate. "Do you think Inindu is right about the Sphere not protecting those who enter the Torment?"

"No!" Maldinado responds a little too quickly.

"One thing's for certain." Hintor accepts his plate back from Nataline. "Everyone will be praying a little more come morning."

"No doubt you'll be the lone holdout." Maldinado says.

"You pray enough for the both of us." Hintor grins, but it suddenly disappears. "You *are* still praying for me, aren't you?"

Maldinado shrugs his shoulders. "Now that I'm protecting the Adow I don't have as much time as I did before. It's hard to fit you in."

Hintor appeals to Nataline, but she motions toward the dishes. "I've been a little busy, myself."

"Tasa Ro! Both of you plotting against me? Really?" Hintor leans back in resignation. "I don't even know how to pray…" Then a thought occurs to him and he unexpectedly slams the table. "Breline!" He points in triumph. "I still have your mother praying for me."

"One of these days you'll actually have to pray for yourself." Maldinado says.

Hintor fills his mouth with a spoonful of pudding and smiles in response.

~

After dinner, DK Vel and Beah are sent to clean up the mess inside the kitchen. They're grateful for the respite from wind and cold. DK Vel looks with envy at the food on the table. He hasn't eaten all day. Not for two days. He and Beah had split a loaf of bread between them—one they sneaked from a basket they were delivering to the Adow.

He twirls his finger through a glob of pudding, puts it to his mouth. Sucks the pudding out from under his fingernail. Beah elbows him in the ribs. A guard is coming down the hallway. The warrior ducks his head into the kitchen. He's wearing Adarian armor, though, neither boy recognizes him. He leaves with a curious glance, but doesn't say a word.

"That was close." Beah says.

"I'm so hungry."

"Then tell me a story about Dsal Tiger. It will take your mind off the hunger while we work." Beah begins gathering the dishes.

"Alright." DK Vel grabs a wooden bucket and a brush from the corner of the kitchen. "Listen to these warnings, and may Dsal guide you to the Sphere:

Dsal Tiger is hunting. He moves his paws over and into the snow drifts littered with fallen limbs from trees long since barren and frozen in death. His fur is heavy, and gathers in clumps around his legs and chest. Only the soft crunch of the snow tracks his path as he moves through the graveyard of trees.

He sees another set of footprints. His eyes narrow. He nestles his belly down into the snow. There is no sign of his prey. He follows the footprints until he finds a cricket hanging upside down from one leg attached to a tree limb. "What do I hunt, cricket? Tell me, and I will not eat you."

"You hunt what follows. You hunt what leads," says the cricket. "You hunt Sumatran."

"Then Sumatran will fill my belly," Dsal Tiger says. "You will live another day, cricket."

Dsal Tiger leaves the cricket and follows the tracks. Snow begins to fall lightly even as a rumbling moves from his stomach to his throat. He sniffs the ground—the trail is fresh, but his prey remains ahead of him. He moves his paws over and into the snow drifts littered with fallen limbs from trees long since barren and frozen in death. His fur is heavy, and gathers in clumps around his legs and chest. Only the soft crunch of the snow tracks his path as he moves through the graveyard of trees.

He sees another set of footprints. He follows the footprints until he finds a cricket hanging upside down from one leg attached to a tree limb. "What do I hunt, cricket? Tell me, and I will not eat you."

"You hunt what follows. You hunt what leads. You hunt Sumatran following Sumatran."

"Then two Sumatrans will fill my belly!" Dsal Tiger declares. "You will live another day, cricket."

Dsal Tiger leaves the cricket and follows the tracks. Unseen behind him, a Rorne tribesman—his torso painted with blood he took from the bear and the lion—emerges from hiding. He leaves no footprints. There is no sound as he approaches the cricket. His hand encloses around the cricket. He raises his hand to his mouth and eats his victim. The tribesman looks down at the tracks of Dsal Tiger in the snow and smiles. Then he transforms himself into a red cricket and waits for Sumatran.

Dsal Tiger sees another set of footprints; now three altogether. He sniffs at the air. He quickens his pace. The snow is falling heavily, now. Snowflakes cover his back. He follows the footprints until he finds a red cricket hanging upside down from one leg attached to a tree limb. "What do I hunt, cricket? Tell me, and I will not eat you."

"You hunt what follows. You hunt what leads," the red cricket says. "You hunt Sumatran following Sumatran following Sumatran."

"Then three Sumatrans will fill my belly," Dsal Tiger says. "You will live another day, cricket."

Dsal Tiger passes by the red cricket even as the red cricket transforms back to the Rorne tribesman. The tribesman pulls a knife from his waist, jumps upon Dsal Tiger's back, and buries the blade into Dsal Tiger's belly. The fight is over quickly. The hunt is finished. Sumatran has fallen. The Rorne tribesman smears the blood of Dsal Tiger upon his chest, lifts Dsal Tiger onto his shoulders, and departs from the path the Sumatran followed.

Beah smiles as DK Vel finishes his story, but it's quickly replaced by a frown. Inindu is standing in the doorway.

Horse and topi, two totally separate creatures yet undeniably united together. The presence of the horse filling the doorway is as overwhelming as the beauty of the topi standing just inside the kitchen. Beah whispers to his friend and DK Vel freezes at the sight of the creature who took Lay'I from him in the streets of Adarian.

"I've been watching you, taggle." The horse speaks the words without a trace of emotion. "You're the one from Adarian–the one with the baby."

"It wasn't me." DK Vel stares at the ground. "I serve Hintor of the Adarian 45th."

"Don't be afraid, boy. I won't hurt you."

"It wasn't me." The taggle insists.

"Don't worry, I'll look after her." Inindu ignores his comment. "Besides, I tend to have a soft spot for anyone my sister curses, though in truth there's been so many I've lost count. Still, it's easy to keep track of the more obvious curses, and cutting off a chunk of someone's ear certainly qualifies. What is your name, boy?"

"DK Vel."

"Come with me, DK Vel. The Adow has suffered greatly in her education, and it's time she learned a few lessons. She has need of a storyteller."

Beah and DK Vel exchange looks of confusion. Inindu doesn't wait for a response. She backs away from the doorway and down the hall past the mumbling, blind topi with the expectation that DK Vel follow, which he does. When she reaches the stairs, Inindu climbs them without making a sound. It is a strange sight, for whereas the taggle creaks with every new step he takes, Inindu moves as though gliding up the staircase. Indeed, the taggle struggles to match her pace.

"Open the door, Faunride." She commands the warrior beside a closed wooden door. "I have a gift for our Adow."

Faunride hesitates, torn between his desire to not disturb the Adow and his fear of Inindu. He knocks on the door and opens it slightly. "My Adow, Inindu is here to see you."

"There's no need to announce her, Faunride. It wouldn't stop her, anyway." The Adow responds.

Inindu pushes past the guard. "That's true."

DK Vel is standing at the top of the stairs, visibly shaking, afraid to enter the Adow's presence for fear of death.

"Come along, boy." Inindu beckons. Faunride gives him a glaring look, but he doesn't prevent the taggle from entering the Adow's chamber.

"I expected Maldinado to be with you." Inindu says with mock surprise.

"That wouldn't be proper." Faunride retorts from the doorway.

Inindu looks back at the guard. "Are you still here? Ayson, are you really that incapable of protecting your

God of Another World: The Adow

Adow?"

"Faunride is my most trusted guard, Inindu." Ayson responds from beside a four post bed covered by a dusty, orange and brown quilt.

"Yes, but he isn't Maldinado now is he, my Adow?"

"You can tell me what you have to say in front of Faunride." The Adow's response is a bit tart.

"No, I can't. I actually have need of Maldinado. I have news of his missing scouts."

"You found them?" Faunride asks.

"Go, fetch Maldinado." Inindu commands. "If you do it quickly I may tell you all about it."

The Adow motions to Faunride who leaves without further comment.

"In the meantime," Inindu continues. "I've brought you a gift, my Adow. He's a storyteller, or as you like to call them, a taggle. Come boy, tell us a story before these walls collapse and Ayson is forced to run and hide for fear of death." Inindu moves to one side of the room, leaving DK Vel with a makeshift stage area, but the room is small– made smaller by Inindu's presence.

"What would you like to hear, my Adow?" The taggle is still shaking, unable to conceal his fear.

"Stand tall, boy." Inindu encourages. "She won't hurt you as long as I'm here."

"That's enough, Inindu." The Adow scolds. "He's scared to death."

"Tell us one of your stories about the tiger." Inindu commands.

The Adow's reaction to the request is a mixture of surprise and fury. Her presence consumes the room, obliterating everyone else as though they were gnats in the wind, even Inindu. DK Vel lowers his eyes, unsure if he should speak or run. If the taggle feared for his life before, he is now certain he will die at her next command. Surprisingly, she says nothing. Everyone is waiting for him to tell a story. He tries to think of one, but his only thought is the image of his severed head rolling on the floor.

"Tell us the one I heard in the kitchen." Inindu persists.

Thankfully, the story comes flooding back. DK Vel begins his tale, nervous at first; his whole body still rattling uncontrollably.

He begins, "Listen to these warnings, and may Dsal guide you to the Sphere: Dsal Tiger is hunting. He moves his paws over and into the snow drifts littered with fallen limbs from trees…" The Adow stares at him with unmistakable horror. The boy isn't sure if he should continue. Luckily, Faunride returns with Maldinado in tow and the taggle is quickly forgotten.

The Madar bows, "My Adow."

"I sent for you," Inindu begins. "I found your scouts. Their bodies were discovered near the blacksmith's forge. He thinks they were killed by a stranger who stayed with him a few days ago. Hasn't seen the stranger, since. Quite the character—offered me broth and beer. You should meet him sometime."

"Another assassin!" Maldinado processes the information. "My Adow, we need to act quickly."

"I agree." Faunride steps in front of the Madar.

~

In the large room downstairs, the assassin waits.

The old topi in the hallway mutters, "'Tis a wraith, 'tis a wraith…"

There's commotion upstairs and soon after Maldinado calls for Hintor. Faunride shouts orders to the Adowian Guards. Warriors quickly appear and await instruction.

"We need to move the Adow!" Ayson shouts.

The Adow is led down the stairs into the hallway below where warriors cram together. Guards surround her, all but suffocate her. Candles are lit in every room revealing barren walls but no assassin. Warriors enter through the front door, squeeze into the hallway to receive their orders, and exit through the back door. Wind blows through the crowded hallway, adding to the noise and confusion.

The assassin moves into the crowd. He draws his sword–everyone is drawing their sword.

"Someone find Teyo!" Faunride shouts.

"Hintor!" Maldinado calls.

The Adow is surrounded by Ayson, Maldinado, and Faunride, but the undeterred assassin moves ever closer, following two warriors who are ordered into the kitchen to secure the food stores. The assassin brushes past Faunride. He'll have to split Maldinado and Ayson who are standing with the Adow directly behind them. She is younger than he imagined. Shorter, too.

A figure appears on the staircase. A flash of magenta catches the assassin's eye. He looks up in time to see Inindu's hair stretching toward him. Her hair, the long magenta hair of Inindu reaches for him and wraps around him. Her hair extends out over the staircase with a wild rage he can barely comprehend.

She lifts the assassin into the air, above the warriors in the hall below. Inindu continues to bind the assassin with her hair until he is completely hidden from view–a spider wrapping her prey.

Then death.

Inindu's hair unravels, revealing emptiness. Her hair retracts like a snake slithering up her arm. Then it falls silent as though no longer alive. Her hair hangs over her shoulders as normal, though every warrior in the hallway below would swear otherwise.

She moves down the steps. "You may want to draw your sword next time we have an assassin in our midst, Ayson. The Adow doesn't need anymore scars."

Inindu exits through the front door, the blind old topi is no longer muttering in the corner of the hallway.

"Who is she?" The Adow asks.

DK Vel collapses at the top of the stairs. He knows who she is…the stories. The ones Beah told him. The stories that aren't often told, and when they are spoken their always told in secret. Morlac has many assassins, but the Sphere only has one. Inindu is the First Assassin.

a taggle's tale

As spoken by a taggle woman to her five children. A baby screamed in her arms, blood flowing from the tips of his ears where they were carved into by the sword of a warrior–the guardian of the Stycral dallic. She held the boy to her breast, but he refused to nurse. The other children were frightened, just as they had been after similar rituals following the birth of their taggle brothers and sisters. So she told them a story, speaking loudly, and rocking the baby back and forth until finally he fell asleep. Her name was Penrem, a woman who gave me shelter one evening. Her brother survived the Torment, only to die two days after his return, beaten by the same guardian who had just carved into her baby's ears. She spoke in the manner of all taggles, for our story is a journey we share. May the Sphere forgive our mother and remember our father, as revealed in Dsal's vision.

— DK Vel

"'T is a feast the Dragon be having tonight, boy."

Hiate and Edran stand atop the roof of the blacksmith shop watching the Adowian Army leave town. The rooftop offers them a reprieve from the dust, if not the wind, and it's cooler than the forge below. The army is an endless procession of armored warriors marching through the streets of Caduum into the Torment. The pass, known as Dragon's Tongue, is steep, but the footing is solid.

"Yer trying to scare me into staying." Edran says.

"'Tis an illusion of glory they seek," Hiate says. "But I fear they're heading toward nothing more than a bitter end." He looks around at Caduum. "Though not as bitter as what we be living here."

"We'll need a banner."

"I'll leave such matters to you."

"I've fashioned one with the symbol of a hammer."

"Have you now? 'Tis a good symbol, to be sure." Hiate places his hand on Edran's shoulder. "And what say the others? Will anyone from Caduum be joining us?"

"No." Edran admits.

"We be on our own, then. Fair enough." Hiate nods as he scratches at his red beard. "We'll need the extra blankets from the house, I think. I'll fetch them. Hurry yerself with the horses."

They descend an iron ladder attached to the side of the blacksmith shop. Edran runs off toward a stall around the back of the stone building, but Hiate pauses just outside the open doorway to the shop. The forge is aglow, evidence of his early morning work. A metal bucket of dragon's ore sits on the dirt floor beside an unopened iron chest. Several hammers and two sets of tongs hang from a small stone pillar which supports the blacksmith's anvil. His leather apron, along with Edran's, hangs from a metal post just inside the doorway. The ties of the apron blow in the wind. Hiate looks down at his calloused hands, rubs them against his chest, and turns toward the house.

Moments later, blacksmith and taggle ride through the streets of Caduum at a steady cantor, their faces all but hidden behind tightly wrapped scarves. Their red hair flows freely behind them, the shock of color suppressed by the dust-filled and swirling gusts. The horses jostle the reigns, snorting constantly, but they continue their pace.

At the bottom of Dragon's Tongue, near the edge of town, Hiate and Edran catch up to the Adowian Army, or rather a horde of taggles trailing after the Adowian Army. Hiate dismounts, retrieves a blanket from behind his saddle, and moves to walk beside the nearest taggle boy. He's naked aside from the brown breechcloth around his waist. No shoes. His hands shield his face against the wind.

"What be yer name, boy?" Hiate shouts. The taggle boy stares at the blacksmith. "'Tis a blanket and horse I offer you. All I ask in return is yer name."

The taggle bows. "I can't accept such gifts of honor, master."

"Then you have no name?"

"My name is Beah, master."

"Beah…'tis a good name. Beah, take the blanket."

Beah stares at the red-haired blacksmith a moment longer. Then he takes the blanket and wraps it around his shoulders. Its wool fibers stab at his wind-burned skin.

"We're falling behind." Edran shouts.

Hiate lifts Beah onto his brown steed and leads the horse forward until they catch up to another taggle. The blacksmith offers her a blanket, as well–in exchange for her name: Lyshmee. And then another taggle: Penrem. And another: Vitrec. Hiate and Edran climb the mountain pass collecting taggles, wrapping them in blankets.

"Why aren't you with the rest of the army?" Beah asks from the saddle.

"It seemed proper we bring up the rear." Hiate scratches at his beard. "Since we be the last ones to join the quest."

"I like you." Beah states.

Chad Michael Cox

Hiate gently pats the boy's leg. "Yer a fine boy, Beah. I like you, too."

Hundreds of taggles climb the mountain around the blacksmith and his apprentice. The Adowian Army marches ahead of them, led by the Adow and her First Etabli. Gone is the dust of Caduum below, but the wind remains. It flows down the mountain pass, growing more frigid as the army ascends.

The journey is slowed by exhaustion. Warriors, marching under the weight of full armor, fight against the burn and growing stiffness in their legs. Every step weighs a thousand pounds. They begin peeling off layers. Those who are mounted are forced to dismount and lead their horses for fear of trampling those on foot. The air is thin. The wind swipes every desperate breath. By the time the First Etabli gives the command to halt for the night, the army is just under halfway up the pass.

The Adow's tent is valiantly erected, the wind, more than once, thwarting the efforts of the taggles selected for the task. Ayson stands uncomfortably, speaking, or rather, shouting with Faunride and Maldinado.

"What's the report?"

Faunride, forced to yell above the drumming of the canvas, proceeds to tell the First Etabli and Maldinado that the fortifications of the camp were abandoned for fear of losing or damaging the other tents. "Only the Adow's tent stands!" Faunride shouts. "The torches make it visible throughout the camp, and it brings comfort to the warriors to know that the Adow is undeterred by the winds of the Torment!"

"Will it hold through the night?" Maldinado asks skeptically.

"It will hold." Faunride responds tersely.

God of Another World: The Adow

"All the same…" Ayson shouts. "Add some more ropes!"

Faunride leaves with a bow and a curious glance as Maldinado walks over to where the Adow sits staring at a game of 5-Ruby.

"The Begn ruby is naked!" The Madar shouts over the wind. "Here, let me show you!" He sits opposite her and proceeds to re-align the rubies. "It's easier to learn the game with the traditional beginning."

"What?" the Adow yells.

The Madar waves his hand and moves the rubies until they are aligned correctly. Then he points to the game in triumph: "Easier!"

"You just ruined my game!" the Adow says.

Maldinado is dumbfounded. "That's not how you play 5-Ruby."

"What?"

"That's not how you play 5-Ruby!"

The Adow waves her hand and moves the rubies until they are where they were before. "Easier!"

Maldinado stares at the game. "It will be over in two moves!"

"I know!" the Adow says. "And I'm going to win!"

Maldinado looks to Inindu for support, but she is sitting behind the Adow brushing her mane and showing no interest in their discussion. All of her attention is focused on a taggle boy who is telling her a story. He turns back to the Adow. "That's cheating!"

"It's manipulation," the Adow declares. "Cheating implies that I have broken the rules of the game—which I haven't. I am simply manipulating the rubies to represent their future state!"

"Do you even know how to play?" he asks.

"All I need to know is how to win. I've watched enough games to know that!"

Maldinado smiles as a thought occurs to him. "Then you also know it's honorable to place a wager before the tusks are thrown."

"What's your wager, Madar?" the Adow shouts.

"No movement on the next throw!" Maldinado removes five gold pieces from a small, leather pouch at his waist and places them before her.

"I don't want your gold."

"Then what shall I wager?"

"If there is no movement this turn, I will double your gold. If there *is* movement…" She checks to make sure no one is watching. "…kiss me." She whispers under the wind.

Maldinado stares at his Adow. The masks are gone. There's no mistaking who she is—and who *he* is. Maldinado glances quickly at Inindu who is still preoccupied with the taggle. Ayson has his back turned. Maldinado looks down at the rubies. There won't be movement. It takes years of practice to throw the tusks in the right pattern…the odds are against it. He looks at the Adow and nods.

She smiles and picks up the three tusks from the dirt. Their eyes meet…her beautiful green eyes. Maldinado watches her throw the boar tusks. They hit the dirt and tumble in an awkward manner. The pattern is wrong. No movement. She stands and walks away from him to open a small chest, returning with a handful of gold. She opens her hand, allowing the coins to fall on the ground around him. He doesn't move. He can't. He's staring at her perfect lips. A kiss offered…

The tent is torn away—taken by the wind.

Without thinking, Maldinado wraps himself around the

God of Another World: The Adow

Adow and bears her to the ground, protecting her with his body. Wind swirls around them, ripping the tent from the pegs that secure it. The Madar watches through the chaos that surrounds him as canvas, rope, bedding, furniture, food and clothing are suddenly pulled into the air. The torches are vanquished, replaced by a howling darkness.

Maldinado lies on top of the Adow, his face against her throat. His nose in her dust-scented hair. There's a flurry of activity around them, but all he can focus on his her pulse against his cheek. Her hands move slowly through his hair. Someone is shouting in the darkness. Her lips…

She pulls him into a kiss.

Then pushes him away as Ayson and Faunride appear.

"Maldinado!" It's Hintor's voice. He was at the back of the tent with Nataline. They were preparing an almond stew.

"Over here!" Maldinado allows Faunride to pull the Adow from his grip. He gets to his knees, grinning despite himself. *She kissed me!*

~

Further down the mountain, the Adow's tent crashes with terrifying surprise. Then it's gone, blown again into the night. Hiate and his small band of taggles, still recovering from the shock, watch it fly overhead.

"'Tis a wraith." He says. "Nothing more. Finish yer story, Beah."

Beah pulls the blanket tighter around his shoulders, and starts again.

The words of the Sphere came to fruition. The topis filled the land. They explored until they found other topis. They developed villages, towns, and cities. They formed alliances, and discovered enemies. Wars began. Warriors were born. To mark the battles, the topis created a calendar.

Fifty-one years later, Inindu waits for a sorcerer to open the door to his home. Though the Sphere hasn't spoken to her since the day of her creation, she clearly heard His voice this morning when she saw the sorcerer in the market square.

"Kill him." The voice was gone as suddenly as it came.

The sorcerer lives alone. He opens the door to find the magenta-haired Inindu standing before him. He's dumbstruck...forgets his magic. He's defenseless before her beauty. Her hair flashes and he dies. She kills him: Erog 23, Completion of the Purple Moon 51. It's her first assassination. He was a sorcerer, a clumsy fool who found power, if not knowledge, in his magic. She leaves no trace of his body.

"Well done." The Sphere's voice affirms.

Five years later she kills her second sorcerer. And again three years later when she kills an unsuspecting merchant turned sorcerer. Then the topis abandon magic in their search for knowledge. Sorcerers become scholars. The Sphere's voice is a constant companion as she kills hundreds of scholars, single-handedly driving them into hiding. They are replaced by topis skilled at politics, ones who neglect their search for knowledge in favor of status. The Adow adorns these new Scholars with purple robes, making them easy for Inindu to identify, but they don't possess the power of the scholars who fled.

Inindu ignores them. She hunts after the true scholars. But the scholars are newly cautious in their learning. They know there is an assassin and they trust no one...except Inindu. Her knowledge attracts them. Her knowledge of the beginning of time. When they see Inindu, they see an opportunity to further their own understanding. She was there! At the beginning, when the Sphere created the land. She was there! They long to hear her stories, but only the taggles tell stories. Inindu shares nothing. Her hair flashes and they die. They all die...except Inindu. She is eternal.

Hiate scratches at his beard. "'Tis a frightening story, Beah."

"Is she really an assassin?" Vitrec asks.

God of Another World: The Adow

"There's nothing to fear, Vitrec. Inindu won't kill a taggle." Edran answers.

"How do you know?" Penrem asks.

Lyshmee, the only taggle girl sitting with the group, shakes her head in disgust. "Why would she? None of us will live long enough for her to bother with. Besides, have you ever heard tale of a taggle who is more powerful than a sorcerer, or could outthink a scholar?"

~

On another part of the mountain, far away from the group of taggles, Inindu shields DK Vel from the wind— her hair stretched and wound tightly around him. The boy can hardly breathe, afraid she will kill him the same way she killed the assassin in Caduum.

THE ADOW

What the hell are we doing in the Torment? What are we searching for? We're at the top of the pass, now what? There is only one way for this to end. Everyone dies. The Arms of the Sphere are never found because they don't exist! This is how I'll be remembered?

Ayson takes my hand.

He's been my salvation these last three days. He understands what I'm facing better than anyone. He had the same feelings at Quel, wanting to run away. My mother looking at him, believing in him, just like Maldinado looks at me. The Madar doesn't understand what I'm asking him to do, and my mother didn't understand what she put Ayson through.

The top of Dragon's Tongue is a valley of balor trees leading toward red-toned peaks in the distance. The balor tree, with its black leaves, is the only known tree in the Torment. Ayson moves his horse forward ahead of me. Inindu follows. Maldinado. Faunride. My entire army. At least the wind has turned into a light breeze, and it isn't as cold as I was expecting. The sun shines brightly overhead leaving only a few pockets of snow to welcome us to Dragon's Torment.

"What keeps the Sphere from entering the Torment?" Hintor asks Inindu.

"Or Morlac from leaving?" Nataline adds.

"Nothing." Inindu responds. "I said Morlac built the Torment to keep the Sphere away. I didn't say it worked."

I've never seen anything like Dragon's Torment. The balor leaves, initially appearing black, shimmer and change color in the breeze. The ground is red dirt with occasional boulders; also red.

"Where's the nearest water source?" Maldinado asks.

Inindu points toward the peaks. "Five days to the north if we live that long."

"Are we in danger of attack?" Faunride reaches for his sword.

"The scholars live here. They call themselves the Rorne tribes. They'll know by now that we've entered their land." Inindu runs her hand through her hair which slithers over and around her fingers.

Faunride and Maldinado both motion to their respective warriors. Faunride and the Adowian Guard fan out to my left. Maldinado and the Adarian 45th flank my right. Hintor moves closer to Nataline. Ayson, still holding my hand, draws his sword.

"Do you even know how to use that thing, Ayson?" Inindu asks.

My First Etabli doesn't respond. I suppose I should respond for him, but I don't feel like getting into it with Inindu, right now. We've been swallowed by the trees. The red peaks, the sun…I can't see anything beyond twenty yards. The Rorne could be anywhere, hiding, waiting to attack the strangers who have entered their land uninvited.

I see an eagle between the leaves overhead. It's the first sign of life I've seen since we entered the Torment. It's a welcome sight. Something normal. "Are there cities in the Torment?" I've always thought of the Torment in terms of desolation. The eagle makes me wonder what kind of world Morlac has made for himself. Surely he would create something similar to what the Sphere created.

"Yes, but we are a long way from the land of Morlac." Inindu answers.

"Do the Rorne ever cross into our world?" Nataline asks.

I never thought about the need to safeguard our borders. I suddenly realize how little I know about Dragon's Torment. Lack of knowledge seems to be a recurring theme, lately.

Inindu smiles with that grin of hers that tells me she knows more than what she's letting on. "The Rorne wouldn't dare enter Caduum." It's the same look she had when she presented that storyteller. The taggle boy who never leaves her side. He's walking next to her, now.

I wish Inindu would just come out and say she knows what I'm doing rather than wielding her storyteller like a sword. She keeps him close–as if to threaten me, but he's only told the one Dsal Tiger story. Maybe he doesn't know any more. Maybe he doesn't know the story Troq told me about the five wolves–the reason for all of this! Whatever he knows, he's staring at me.

"What's your name?" It seems important. I want to know my accuser's name.

God of Another World: The Adow

"DK Vel." The boy responds with bowed head.

"This is hardly the time for introductions, my Adow." Inindu says. The wind has finally dissipated, but I swear her hair is in constant motion. I never noticed it before she killed the assassin, or swallowed him, or whatever it is she did to him, but her hair hasn't stopped moving since! As if tasting the air in search of another victim.

"You gave him to me as a present, remember? Though you've kept him all to yourself!" She has! Not that I care… but maybe I should.

Why did Troq tell me taggle stories?

"How many Dsal Tiger stories do you know, DK Vel?" Why am I letting this taggle rule over me? So what if he knows about the five wolves, no one will make the connection between his story and my prophecy. Go ahead, DK Vel. Tell your stories!

Ayson turns in his saddle. "If we're heading into an ambush, I'd rather he didn't tell a story."

"Answer me, taggle." I let go of Ayson's hand.

"I've never counted them, my Adow." DK Vel responds.

"My guardian used to tell me a story about a tiger who hunted after five wolves. Do you know it?" So there it is out in the open, but if Inindu and her storyteller know anything they're keeping their emotions to themselves.

"Yes, I know the tale, my Adow."

The impact of his confession is anything but crushing. Not in the sense I was expecting, anyway. Memories of Troq holding me, telling me stories while I fell asleep; they come with crippling force. Tasa Ro! My eyes fill with tears, but I manage to keep them from running down my face like a blubbering fool.

"Tell me that story." My voice is quivering.

Chad Michael Cox

Ayson catches the change in tone, but I don't care. I want to hear Troq's story one more time. Inindu gives me a curious look. Fine! Stare! Everyone, look at me!

The taggle begins his tale, but it isn't his voice I hear, the boy's soft pitch is replaced by Troq's deeper tones. His face–that white beard. I close my eyes, trying not to have a complete breakdown on the doorstep of Dragon's Torment. Troq drove me here with his story. I can almost feel his arms around me. The boy's tale is exactly the same, as though Troq memorized it from a taggle.

Why did you tell me taggle stories, Troq? But I'm glad he did, and I'm glad Inindu has brought this storyteller into my life. Her efforts to trap me be damned!

"A tiger in Dragon's Torment searching for five wolves." Inindu comments after DK Vel finishes his story. "Strikingly similar to our own situation."

Trapped! I wipe the tears from my eyes and turn to face my accuser, but Inindu isn't looking at me. She's staring at the eagle overhead. There are now five eagles circling our position. They're flying together. Circling together.

"That's odd." Ayson notes.

Maldinado emerges from the trees. My great and beautiful warrior. "Is everything alright?" He notices the tears in my eyes.

"Yes, what did you find?" Ayson answers, not realizing the Madar was speaking past him.

I nod. Yes, everything is alright, Maldinado. Why wouldn't it be? You worship me, and I've led you to your death. What could possibly be wrong? I want to kiss you and run from you all at once. Take me! No, I can never be yours! Tasa Ro!

"More trees." Maldinado answers. "But if there's anyone out there we'll find them."

God of Another World: The Adow

Faunride returns. My future First Etabli. He looks at me with the same look Maldinado gave me. The same question, "Is everything alright?"

No, nothing is right! Troq is dead and I'm in the Torment. Are you blind? We're all going to die and it's my fault. I've led you here. I've led you to your death.

Ayson grabs my hand, once more. Squeezes it until I'm breathing again.

a taggle's tale

As spoken by an old taggle man at the request of his son. The man spoke deeply, almost too low, but there was warmth in his voice and the boy listened intently. The man motioned sparingly, typically pointing in the distance, or tracing a circle above his head. His name was my name. I spoke in the manner of all taggles, for our story is a journey we share. May the Sphere forgive our mother and remember our father, as revealed in Dsal's vision.

- DK Vel

Maldinado leads the Adarian 45th through the balor trees. He looks skyward, a habit he's developed over the past two days. What started as one eagle has grown to at least sixty circling above them.

"They're more annoying than Brink!" Birate grumbles from atop his horse. He looks ahead to where the banner bearer of the Adarian 45th rides. "At least *he* disappears when I close my eyes!" He closes his eyes to further test the theory then opens them again with a curse directed toward the eagles. "Tasa Ro! Go find a fish, or something!"

Aside from the birds, however, the warriors have found

no other signs of life. The Adarian 45th is an hour ahead of the Adow and her army, and at least two hundred yards to the right of Faunride and the Adowian Guard. If the Rorne tribes are waiting in ambush, as Inindu suggested, they are well disguised and patient.

Maldinado feels the horse lurch as it begins climbing a good-sized hill. The forest terrain has been steep this morning as they move out of the valley where they spent most of the previous day. He checks on the eagles. The brown birds fly together, circling the sky like a whirlpool.

"I've never seen anything like it." Gan-Pi, a pimpled face warrior, rides beside his Rovet and Madar, a position normally reserved for Hintor who remains with the Adow in order to better protect Nataline.

Maldinado nods. "I get the feeling we'll see a lot of strange things before this quest is over."

The Adarian 45th climb through the trees in spread formation, cresting the hill to discover a small village nestled within a clearing in the forest. The warriors draw their swords and close in on the village. There is no movement, however, for the village has long since been abandoned. The shelters, made from tiger skins that have been stretched and sewn together, surround a single balor tree that serves as the village centerpiece. There is something odd about the tree, but Maldinado cannot make it out from this distance.

The warriors search the empty shelters, finding nothing of value. Maldinado moves toward the balor tree, drawn by the strange shapes hanging from the limbs. What is that? He reins in his horse and stares at the balor tree in disbelief. Every leaf is the feather of an eagle. Every limb bears the skull of an eagle. Severed talons hang like fruit. It has been so carefully constructed that the balor tree has become the sculptured home of a thousand eagles. Something shudders at the top of the tree and a living eagle ascends into the sky, joining the whirlpool of birds above the clearing.

Gan-Pi shoots an arrow at the eagle, but it falls harmlessly.

Maldinado sheathes his sword. He slaps at something crawling on his neck, a red cricket that jumps onto his leg. Maldinado flicks it away and motions for the warriors to keep moving.

"Gan-Pi! Report back to the Adow. Tell her about this village." Maldinado orders. He takes one last look at the tree of eagles; then skyward at the circling birds. "May the Sphere be with us."

~

"And keep us in His light." Teyo completes Faunride's prayer.

The two Adowian Guards watch the birds a second longer before returning their focus to the forest.

"Look!" Teyo points to his left where an orange tiger walks parallel to their position.

"Valin!" Faunride calls. A thin, but able warrior moves forward. "Our supper has arrived."

Valin rides away with an arrow notched in his bow. The entire Adowian Guard, marching in a procession, stops to watch the hunt. The archer takes aim, releasing the arrow while remaining perfectly balanced upon his horse. It strikes one of the trees, sending the startled tiger back into the depths of the forest.

The warriors cackle and holler at the failed attempt to kill the tiger. Valin rides back to the procession hanging his head in shame. The Adowian Guard continues its march through the balor trees, shouting insults toward Valin and boasting how they would have killed the tiger if given the chance.

Teyo taps Faunride on the arm. "He's back."

"Yla! See what you can do." Faunride calls.

The warriors cheer the new hunter as he approaches the tiger with great enthusiasm. He dismounts to draw his bow, but the tiger moves at the last minute causing the arrow to sail wide. Yla shoots another arrow, but the tiger disappears into the forest. Yla returns under a chorus of insults.

The game continues when the tiger returns. Another warrior fails. Teyo is sent next, but even the master archer cannot slay the beast. No longer amused, Faunride orders the guard to dismount and draw their bows. They wait, more than a few stealing glances at the still circling birds overhead. Their squawking pierces the silence, one after another as though taking turns.

Finally the tiger appears from behind the trees. Faunride gives the signal and hundreds of arrows fill the sky, slapping pass balor leaves or penetrating tree bark with a thud, but none of the arrows hit their mark. The tiger is unharmed.

At least seven warriors draw their swords and charge after the animal, followed by another dozen. The entire Guard yells after them, cheering their efforts.

"We'll get him, now!" Faunride yells with enthusiasm.

Teyo flicks a red cricket off his arm.

~

"I've never seen so many crickets." Nataline brushes at her gown.

Hintor points to the forest floor. "They're everywhere."

Ayson looks up at the eagles circling overhead. "There must be a hundred of them now. I've never seen so much as one eagle at a time."

"The Torment used to be desolate." Inindu says. "It appears Morlac has added some seasoning to his world." Inindu reaches with her hair toward a cluster of crickets. Snagging one, she pulls it closer to inspect its red body, black hindquarters, and long antennae.

"That's a rather disturbing talent you possess, honored Inindu." Nataline says.

She transfers the cricket to her hand, allowing it to jump away. "I have many talents, though none of them include the ability to cook quite so well as you."

"Thank you." Nataline bows her head with gratitude.

"Why would they gather like that?" Ayson is still looking at the birds.

"I wish they would go away." The Adow reaches for the First Etabli's hand.

"I suspect they are the eyes and ears of Morlac." Inindu offers. "Or the Rorne tribes. Yes, they could be connected to the scholars. If that's the case they've gained a great deal of knowledge since last I was here." Inindu sneers with mirth. "You're in luck, Ayson. It turns out you won't have to bother us with your life much longer."

"Not again!" The Adow scolds. "What happened at Quel wasn't his fault!"

Ayson looks back toward his daughter.

"It wasn't your fault." The Adow squeezes his hand.

~

"There!" Beah shouts.

The taggles move through the balor trees on bare feet as quietly as the tiger that now stalks them.

"I see it, boy. There's no need to be shouting." Hiate says.

"I've never seen a tiger before." Edran confesses.

Whispers of *Dsal Tiger* move through the group of taggles.

"'Tis one of them that hunted in Caduum when I was a yearling." Hiate says. "Killed five of us before we finally got him. This one seems bigger than I remember."

"He's amazing." Beah says.

THE ADOW

"Listen!" Ayson pauses.

Silence hums softly in the night. "The birds?"

"They've stopped squawking!"

The silence fails to bring me any comfort. The birds have encircled us for seventeen days; a constant swirling presence overhead–hundreds of them filling the sky. They squawk one after the other, a succession of endless sound that is driving me mad! But now, silence. It's worse than the squawking!

Ayson moves toward the tent opening even as Faunride enters. "First Etabli!"

"I know." Ayson exits the tent with Faunride beside him.

Maldinado moves to protect me, something I find myself resisting. It's bad enough having Ayson around, and Faunride…the Adowian Guard. Now Maldinado and the Adarian 45th surround me. I'm used to being left to fend for myself, used to Ayson cowering behind me. Strange I would miss *that*.

I draw my sword and move in front of the Madar.

Feeling awkward and empowered at the same time. This is where I belong!

"Expecting the birds to attack?" Maldinado mocks.

"Weren't *you*?" I turn on him, my sword still raised.

"Do you threaten all your lovers?" Inindu asks.

That's another thing. Inindu's tone has completely changed with me ever since that taggle boy told his story about the five wolves. I *know* she knows I'm lying. I wish she would accuse me and get it over with instead of taunting me with that added smirk of hers lacing every comment. I wish this quest had never happened! I wish the damn birds would go away and leave me alone!

"Do you suppose they've left?" Nataline asks.

"No." Inindu responds.

Hintor draws his sword, positioning himself to protect Nataline.

"Not you, too?" Maldinado chides.

"I was just following your lead."

Nataline reaches for the long-knife at her side. "I can hear them moving."

I turn around, half expecting an eagle to fly into the tent. I can feel them—a suffocating awareness that the birds are still there. Tasa Ro! I sheath my sword and head outside. Maldinado follows. Of course he follows! He has to protect me after all.

Ayson and Faunride are staring into the sky. I force myself to look. No moon. No stars. Only a swirling darkness. Why aren't they squawking? Tasa Ro! Squawk!

I hear a tiger's roar in the distance. I draw my sword. Maldinado and Faunride both step in front of me. Another roar.

"Why don't they attack?" Faunride asks.

"It's a warning." Inindu emerges elegantly from the tent

as though flaunting her ability to stay calm. "The scholars are telling us to go home. The eagles and tigers are the eyes of the scholars." Inindu reaches for a red cricket with her hair. "The crickets, too."

"Why do they want us to leave?" Ayson asks.

"Because they know they cannot defeat the Adow's Army on their own." Inindu responds. Again with the smirk! "Which means Morlac will be forced to send the Kul, and even the scholars fear the Kul."

"What about you?" Maldinado asks. "Do you fear the Kul?"

Inindu turns to me. Why is she staring at me? "Tell me Madar, have you ever heard the story of Dsal Tiger and the five wolves?"

"He wasn't there when the taggle told it." I respond, daring her to continue. Is this how she wants to accuse me? In front of him? Is this the moment she's been waiting for?

"In the end, the tiger is consumed by the Kul." Her tone is almost playful.

"What does a taggle's tale have to do with anything?" Maldinado asks—oblivious to the game Inindu is playing. What game *is* she playing?

"No, I don't fear the Kul." The playfulness is gone. "In truth I have come to the Torment to kill her...or be killed."

"*Her?*" Faunride asks.

"Her." Inindu confirms.

I never pictured the Kul as a female. Wait! "What about the five wolves?" I ask, assuming Inindu understands my question. I *need* to know if she understands.

"I'll leave that quest to you, my Adow." What the hell does that mean?

"You can be killed?" Ayson interrupts our cryptic conversation.

God of Another World: The Adow

THE ADOW

Inindu is genuinely shocked by the concern in his voice. For that matter, I'm just as shocked. "We all die, Ayson. Some of us later than others. Take you, for example." And she's recovered.

"Have you ever fought the Kul?" Maldinado asks.

"No." Inindu admits. She looks up at the birds. "I think I'll go find that blacksmith from Caduum; see if he has anymore beer and broth. DK Vel tells me he joined our little quest and has been traveling with the taggles." She directs her last comment toward me. "You should meet him sometime."

What about the wolves? Tell me about the wolves! It doesn't matter. She knows and she doesn't care. Why doesn't she care? Tasa Ro! She's as bad as the eagles. Squawk already!

Instead, she walks away, leaving me standing with my three protectors. I sheath my sword and all but run back to the tent, startling Hintor and Nataline who are kissing. It's no longer cute.

"Leave me alone!"

They scramble out of the tent just as my three guardians enter. I'm never alone. I'm completely surrounded, unable to escape, and they'll all die because of me.

~

Five hours later, Troq is holding me in my dreams. I'm sitting in his lap with his arms around me. His white beard hangs over my shoulder and rubs against my cheek. His tobacco breath falls softly upon my forehead. We are sitting in a velvet red chair beside a silent fire. That's odd.

"Pleeease tell me a story." I beg. "I'm not even tired, yet."

"Alright, Ovda. Alright." He kisses my head. "Have I ever told you the story about the tiger that ate a whale?"

Chad Michael Cox

"How can a tiger eat a whale?" I ask.

Troq begins his story, his fingers caressing my arm.

The tiger walks along the cliffs overlooking an ocean. He's waiting. He climbs atop a large rock and stares into the setting sun. He roars as only a tiger can roar, sending dirt and pebbles tumbling from the cliff face into the ocean.

A seagull comes and hovers above him. "What do you wait for, tiger?"

"I wait for what the sun flees. I await the Kul," tiger says.

"Then eat me, for you will need wings to defeat the Kul," the seagull says.

The tiger opens his mouth, and the seagull flies inside, dying without a sound. He swallows the seagull and roars, causing wings to appear on the tiger's back. The sun settles under the horizon, but the Kul doesn't appear.

A ram emerges from the forest behind the tiger. "What do you wait for, tiger?"

"I wait for what the forest hides. I await the Kul," he roars.

"Then eat me, for you will need my horns to defeat the Kul."

The tiger opens his mouth and the ram enters, dying without a sound. He swallows the ram and roars, causing horns to appear on the head of the tiger. The forest behind him shakes in the wind, but the Kul isn't there.

A whale rises to the surface of the ocean, sending spray high into the sky. So high that it reaches the top of the cliff where the tiger paces. "What do you wait for, tiger?"

"I wait for what moves in the ocean. I await the Kul."

"Then eat me, for you will need my strength to defeat the Kul," says the whale.

The tiger opens his mouth and the whale enters, dying without a sound. He swallows the whale and roars, causing his body to double in size. The ocean crashes against the cliff, but the Kul isn't there.

THE ADOW

The tiger awaits the Kul. Sun and Moon disappear. Fire burns in the forest. Ocean waves turn to sand. Still the Kul does not appear. The tiger walks along the cliffs. He climbs a boulder to roar, but the sound is the squawk of a seagull.

"I am the Kul!" The seagull says.

The tiger roars again. It's the bleating of a ram.

"I am the Kul!" The ram says.

The tiger roars again. It's the moan of a whale.

"I am the Kul!" The whale says.

Then the tiger erupts. His body splits in half. Emerging from his remains are the seagull, the ram, and the whale who watch as the tiger falls silently from the cliffs.

~

I wake with the feeling I'm falling. The tent is dark. Ayson lies snoring beside me. Faunride stands guard, his silhouette barely visible against the canvas.

"My Adow?"

"I'm alright, Faunride."

But it's another lie.

Chad Michael Cox

a taggle's tale

As spoken by a taggle boy before the throne of the Adow. He spoke with confidence and with great emotion. His performance was vibrant, at times surprising, and the gathered warriors, along with their Adow, were careful to note every word. Beyond general interest, they were there to learn from the boy, keeping earnest notes. When he finished his tale, the taggle was asked to tell his story again, and again a third time. The boy's name was my own. I spoke in the manner of all taggles, for our story is a journey we share. May the Sphere forgive our mother and remember our father, as revealed in Dsal's vision.

- DK Vel

The magenta horse picks at a pile of red and yellow apples. Inindu, the topi half, drinks a bowl of warm chicken broth, chasing it with lukewarm beer. Behind her is a circle of taggles, including DK Vel, Beah, and Edran. The boys are asleep, huddled in the manner of taggles. Hiate, the blacksmith, sits across from Inindu finishing off his fifth round of broth and beer. The eagles swirl silently above them. The tigers roar in the distance.

"It won't be long." Inindu says.

"'Tis the Kul be causing the eagles to grow silent. They can see what the tigers cannot." Hiate pauses to listen for the gentle screech of the red cricket, but even they are silent. "The crickets too be sensing the presence of the Kul."

"The tiger is always the last to know." Inindu's hair reaches for the broth, the ladle that hangs over the black pot above the fire, filling her bowl before dipping her tankard into an open cask of beer.

"I be creating the tiger for a very specific reason, daughter." Hiate replies. "The tiger 'tis beautiful and independent of this land."

"Like you, dearest father? Is the tiger a representation of the mighty Sphere?"

Hiate scratches at his beard. "The tiger be representing the same as yer beauty, and that of your sister, the Adow."

"A beauty that kills?"

Hiate laughs. "Beauty 'tis a curse to be certain." Hiate drinks the last of his beer. "My father used to tell me life 'tis covered in ashes, and death 'tis decorated with golden jewels." He looks up at Inindu. "No offense meant to yerself."

Inindu smiles knowingly. "You never had a father."

"As true a statement as ever there be. I'm alone. I was alone." He points toward Edran. "The boy keeps me company. The two of us are one family. Just as I created yerself to be one creature made from two. And yer sister. Adow and First Etabli be joined to produce one heir."

"That isn't working out so well." Inindu crunches into another apple.

"She be free to choose her path same as yer free."

"You mean she's free as long as she worships you."

"Not everyone be worshiping me. I hear Morlac has his

share of followers."

"Thanks to me, you mean."

"Thanks to yer decision to ignore me."

"I was busy with Adarian."

"Adarian was never meant to be yers, daughter."

"We agreed not to discuss him, remember?" Inindu says. "And you've ignored me ever since you created me!"

"I haven't ignored you, daughter. You be avoiding me."

"It's not my fault you chose to live in Caduum."

"I wasn't always in Caduum. I be watching you and yer sister since the beginning."

"Yes, her beloved Troq." Inindu reaches for more broth and beer. "I'm surprised she never realized who you were."

"She loves without the need for knowledge."

"She follows without understanding. My sister has never been the brightest star."

"I created her for a very different purpose than yers."

A log shifts in the fire, a loud crack that sends sparks into the air.

Inindu's hair reaches for the blacksmith, wrapping around his red hair, stroking his beard. "Do you find me beautiful, father?"

Hiate pulls her hair away from his face. "In this form I see yer beauty, Inindu, but it does not hide the death within you."

Inindu pulls her hair away. "Then we disgust one another?"

"No, daughter. I still love you."

"Well, I *despise* you." Inindu stands to leave, topi mounting horse. She grins despite herself. "Hiate the blacksmith amuses me, however."

Hiate stands, slightly wobbling as he talks. "Will you face the Kul?"

God of Another World: The Adow

Inindu smirks. "Are you asking me, or is that a command?"

"You be free to choose beautiful creature." Hiate bows with exaggeration.

"Yes, I will face the Kul. And I will hunt Morlac." Inindu heads into the darkness with a final comment mocking his accent. "I be an assassin, after all."

Hiate watches after her, a magenta haze of inebriation. "Did you hear all of that, boy?"

DK Vel doesn't move for fear of discovery.

Hiate sits down to another round of broth and beer. "Come, boy. It's time you stopped living in fear. I'll not be harming you."

DK Vel opens his eyes, but still refuses to move.

"Does it surprise you to know yer god lives his life covered in the ashes of a blacksmith forge? To be certain, I live in places others seldom visit." He lies down on his side. "'Tis the reason I travel with the taggles, no doubt. You be less than desirable, but yer simple and honest creatures."

The taggle boy can't help but think *is he going to kill me?*

"No, boy." Hiate says. "If I kill you there be no one left to tell my story."

The boy sits up, about to say something, but Hiate the blacksmith…Hiate the Sphere is asleep.

The land of Morlac is quiet despite the eagles circling overhead, and the red crickets that crawl everywhere; even the tigers move quietly through the trees.

DK Vel can't sleep. He stares with horror and wonder at the blacksmith…mostly wonder. A sudden peace descends upon him. He leaves the circle of taggles to squat in front of Hiate, leaning forward until his face is equal with his god–the red beard of the Sphere.

Forgive our mother

Remember our father

He prays the prayer several times—only a thought, at first. Then he whispers it, repeats it, growing louder until the blacksmith stirs. Hiate opens his eyes to find the boy's face inches from his own.

"What is it, boy?"

"Forgive our mother, remember our father."

Hiate wraps his arm around the taggle, pulling him down into an embrace. The blacksmith closes his eyes, still on the edge of sleep. "I've never forgotten you, boy. I be in every taggle's tale - guiding you, bringing you comfort…"

The Sphere falls asleep, the boy still in his arms.

~

Three hours later the Rorne attack.

The first to die is Beah. A red cricket crawls over his outstretched fingers, transforming while the boy sleeps. The cricket sheds its form, growing in size until the red exoskeleton is completely replaced by blue skin. Antennae become a nose. A face appears, covered with deep, infected sores—his entire body decaying. Long, black hair gathers on his shoulders, the rest of his body completely shrouded under black robes.

He buries his hand into Beah's body, crushing his heart while he sleeps.

Lyshmee, Penrem, and Vitrec die in quick succession. Their deaths awaken Edran who is startled by the sight of the Rorne tribesman. He backs away in frantic fear until Hiate appears, burying his fist into the tribesman's nose.

"'Tis the wraiths come to fetch your soul, boy!" Hiate smiles at the disfigured form of the tribesman. "These be having scars, though."

More crickets transform. Hiate barrels into them, taking five scholars to the ground. He rolls and stands at the ready. He puts his hands together, swinging his arms like a club at the closest tribesman. He lowers his shoulder and crashes into another group of Rorne, taking three down to the ground.

Then Edran is beside him, handing his master a sword. The apprentice wields his own blade, fully recovered from his initial shock.

DK Vel kneels over the bloodless body of Beah, unaware his friend is dead, desperately trying to wake him. "Beah!"

Hiate lowers his sword into the head of one of the Rorne. There is a look of shock as blood rises to coat the tribesman's face. "'Tis the steel of Caduum, wraith!" Hiate's red beard parts in a vicious grin. "I be killing yer kind since before I could raise the hammer."

He pulls the sword from the tribesman's head. He kills three more Rorne. Edran kills another. Their movements are clunky, but their steel is deadly. The Rorne die—seventeen of them pile around the blacksmith and his apprentice.

Hiate lets another tribesman slide from his sword. Rorne cover the horizon, unveiled by the approaching dawn; thousands of red crickets now transformed and slaughtering the taggles. They're not even fighting. They have nothing to fight *with*.

Hiate drops his sword and moves toward DK Vel. The boy is still kneeling beside Beah's body. Hiate falls to his knees and pulls the yearling into his chest. "Yer friend be dead, boy."

DK Vel nods knowingly. "He asked his uncle for a blessing. He wanted to survive the Torment. He was my friend. Why didn't you save him?"

"He be in a better place now." Hiate kisses and embraces the head of DK Vel. "'Tis a much better place."

Chad Michael Cox

"Why aren't they attacking?" Edran points to the complacent taggles in the distance. "They won't survive!"

"None of them *want* to survive." Hiate looks over the battlefield. "Come, boys. The taggles be finding their peace. 'Tis the Adow be needing us now." He pulls DK Vel to his feet, but the taggle resists. "Alright, boy, I understand. 'Tis an honorable thing to be a friend even in death." Hiate kneels down and lifts Beah's body, cradling him against his chest. "Now hurry and let's be off!"

Edran grabs the reins and steadies the two horses. They mount, Hiate still cradling Beah's body, and leave the taggles, moving through the chaos of the Adowian Army as they rush to meet their enemy. They pass the banners of the Kiel 2nd, the Lull 28th, the Galesh 41st…

"May the Sphere be with us!" Someone shouts.

"He already is!" DK Vel whispers, uncertain what it really means. His friend is dead. That's all he knows.

~

Hiate dismounts and cradles Beah's body once more. He pauses before a forgotten campfire, waiting for Edran and DK Vel to join him. Heat ripples through the air, but the blacksmith doesn't mind. It's cooler than the forge.

"Shouldn't we bury him?" DK Vel asks.

"'Tis a curse to be buried." Hiate insists. "Say yer peace, boy."

DK Vel places his hand upon his friend's head, unsure how to say goodbye. He is familiar with death, but friendship was foreign until now. "May the Sphere forgive our mother."

"And remember our father." Edran adds.

Hiate heaves the body into the flames without further ceremony. "Take yer wraith with you, though. I'll not be having you haunt me, boy." He turns away from the fire.

"We've no time to watch him burn." A healer, whose white robes are covered with blood, approaches as the blacksmith leaves. "'Tis no place for a healer, but I thank you to watch the fire all the same. If I return, burn me quickly. 'Tis a cursed land we roam."

The healer nods with understanding.

Hiate retrieves a spare sword from behind his saddle and turns to DK Vel. He kneels before the boy so he is eye-to-eye with him. "'Tis here we must part. I need you to take this sword to yer master, boy. Can you do that for me?"

The boy nods.

Hiate hands him the sword. "You'll find Hintor in the Adow's tent. 'Tis nothing to fear, boy. The wraiths haven't reached him, yet. Take this to him and tell him Maldinado insists he use Caduum steel. He'll be able to protect you with it." Hiate stands and mounts his horse. "Edran and I have to find the Adow."

With that, the blacksmith and his apprentice leave the taggle standing alone, holding a sword, in the middle of a battlefield. Never did DK Vel envision this when he first left Yenul.

a taggle's tale

As spoken by an old taggle man. This was his last tale, for his voice was hoarse with cough and his body weakened by death. He sat in a wooden chair as his audience gathered close enough to hear his garbled words. His cadence was inconsistent. His wheezing became a distraction. By all accounts his presentation lacked enthusiasm, but it was filled with passion. Those who were there embraced his life, and honored him with their attention. The man's name was DK Vel. He spoke in the manner of all taggles, for his story is a journey we all share. May the Sphere forgive his mother and remember his father, as revealed in Dsal's vision.

- The Adow

Maldinado and the Adarian 45th charge into the Rorne like bears into water. They are a good distance from the rest of the Adowian Army, sent in the night to guard the perimeter while Faunride and the Adowian Guard remained behind to protect the Adow. The Madar sends his sword through the first tribesman he encounters, and the next. Then he reins in, adjusts his breastplate, and searches for another opponent.

An eagle rises.

The Madar sees it out of the corner of his eye, but he quickly buries his sword in the belly of another tribesman.

An eagle rises.

Maldinado hacks downward from atop his horse. He strikes between the head and shoulder of a tribesman. He feels the body collapse under his sword. He shifts and delivers a blow to another tribesman.

An eagle rises.

Maldinado hears a scream, but he doesn't turn. He swings his sword from one Rorne to the next. They aren't fighting back. They don't even resist! He pulls on the reigns. They aren't dead. There aren't any bodies! Their black cloaks lay in circular piles as though the Rorne disrobed and vanished.

An eagle emerges, its head jerks and twists, finally settling its gaze upon Maldinado. The bird gives a threatening squawk, steps away from the cloak, and spreads its massive brown wings.

The eagle rises.

A warrior screams, drawing Maldinado's attention from the sky. The screaming warrior sits awkwardly atop his horse, staring with horror at the rotting blue hand now sticking out the front of his chest. Mounted behind the warrior is the Rorne tribesman who holds the warrior's heart in his hand, veins and arteries still attached.

A warrior dies.

Maldinado swings downward, hacking away at the approaching scholars. Their robes fall to the ground and an eagle rises.

A warrior dies.

Maldinado jumps off his horse to strike at the nearest Rorne. He follows the cloak until it settles, plunging his sword into the mound. The Madar hits his mark, striking the eagle still hidden within thus triggering another transformation. The figure of the tribesman returns. He is dead.

Maldinado swings at another tribesman, again waiting for the eagle to appear.

"Kill the birds!" he yells.

A warrior dies.

Two Rorne extend their hands into-and-through the back of an unsuspecting warrior. He cries out but a third tribesman buries his hand into the warrior's throat effectively muting his scream.

A warrior dies.

The Madar adjusts his helmet, raises his sword, and kills a tribesman. In the distance he sees Brink, the banner bearer of the Adarian 45th. "Lucky bastard!"

The eagles descend.

They fold their wings to better pierce the air and crash into the warriors of the Adarian 45th as if they were nothing more than clouds in the sky. The birds transform after they pass through warrior flesh, emerging on the other side as a fully formed tribesman, their hands and teeth noticeably streaked with blood.

The eagles descend.

A gnarled and twisted hand stretches toward the Madar, but he pulls away. His enemy wears a white, patchy beard. Clumps of it are missing, thus exposing the rotting skin of his blistered face. Maldinado strikes him down and waits for the eagle, but this time a red cricket emerges. Maldinado steps on it.

He searches the horizon for the banner of the Adarian 45th. It still waves in the distance. "Damn you, Brink! Die already!"

Maldinado turns to find Gan-Pi along with Birate and

five other warriors who stand beside him. There is wildness in their eyes from the excitement of battle.

Gan-Pi kisses his sword. "We are in your service, my Rovet."

"For Adarian!" Maldinado shouts.

The eight warriors mount a ferocious and coordinated assault. Two of them strike the scholars while another two wait for the eagles to appear. Two protect the ones who wait, and the final two warriors ward off any eagle attempting to descend. More warriors join them, quickly doubling their number. The assault of the Adarian 45th turns the battle.

Strike! Wait. Kill!

Then the tigers arrive.

Dozens of them move in pack formation. The orange and black tigers leap into the fray and the Adarians die.

Maldinado is slammed to the ground; powerful paws draped over his shoulders, musty fur smashed against his nose. But the tiger convulses and dies. Maldinado rolls and pushes the animal off of him, retrieving his sword from the belly of the tiger even as it transforms.

Adarians die.

Again, he is thrown to the ground. His sword is sent clattering to the rocky terrain. The tiger raises a paw as Maldinado struggles against the weight of the beast. The paw is abruptly severed by little Birty's sword, however. The tiny warrior swings through and returns to bury his sword in the tiger's chest, setting Maldinado free.

"For Adarian!" Birate shouts.

Adarians die.

Maldinado drives his sword into another tiger. He swings downward and cuts into the neck; hacks away until the head is completely severed and the tiger is dead. Then something strikes him in the back of the head. He falls to the ground in a heap.

Adarians die.

He's dizzy…disoriented. He sees a tiger running toward him. The Madar gets to his knees and strikes upward with all that remains of his strength.

Adarians die.

He yanks the sword out and removes his badly damaged helmet. His head is throbbing. All around him the warriors of the Adarian 45th are dying. Mauled. Bloody. Dead. Their bodies surround him. He searches the horizon for the banner of the Adarian 45th, but it's nowhere in sight.

Brink is dead. The banner has fallen.

"May the Sphere be with you…" Maldinado says.

No other banner bearer ever lasted so long.

~

Ayson rides after the Adow. Her black hair, like her mother's, flowing in the wind behind her. Unlike her mother, however, she wields a sword.

"Attack!" The Adow yells. She moves pass the warriors of the Adowian Army, traveling deep into the enemy forces with little regard for her own safety.

Faunride tries to stay with her, but the Rorne close ranks and surround him, halting his progress. He can't reach her to protect her. Ayson is even further away from her.

The Adow is alone.

A moment later, Inindu is beside her.

"Where have you been?" the Adow asks.

"I was talking to our father."

"This is no time to be praying!"

"I can't think of a better time."

"It was all a lie, Inindu!"

"This is no time for a confession, my Adow."

God of Another World: The Adow

"It was a story that Troq used to tell me. This quest is just a story!"

"I know."

The Rorne converge upon them. The Adow raises her sword, striking down the nearest scholar whose body bursts into flames.

"I was beginning to think you'd never learn to use that thing!" Inindu taunts.

Her magenta hair constantly shifts like a pit of vipers. Slide. Weave. Strike! They all die. And she watches with great curiosity, for death must not be ignored, nor does she avoid their eyes. She studies the tightening of the eyelids, and the void that forms in their pupils.

Death is something she'll never experience.

The Adow shows no interest in such things rather she obliterates her enemy. Dozens of dead scholars lay burning at her feet. There is no hesitation in her assault, no pause for death's sake. She swings the sword with a fierceness driven by the guilt she feels. She turns to plunge her blade into another scholar. His body erupts in a blaze.

"My Adow!" Faunride dismounts and sends his sword into the nearest tribesman. The black cloak collapses and he waits for the eagle to emerge, but there is only a red cricket. He steps on it and moves to the next scholar, trying to reach the Adow, but he is pushed away from her. There are too many of them.

Farther back, Ayson has also dismounted only to be surrounded by the Rorne. Their diseased hands reach for him. Red crickets crawl all over him. He swings at everything and nothing. He stomps and jumps, trying to shake the crickets loose. They're everywhere!

There's a sharp pain in his arm causing him to drop his sword. Another source of pain at his side. The Rorne are touching him; hands move inside his body. He can feel their hands! One in his leg. His shoulder. Black cloaks surround him, swirl around him. A finger touches his heart then a hand wraps around his very life. He looks down with a final moment of clarity. The gold of his armor is barely visible. Red crickets cover his body. The hands of the Rorne tighten around his bones, his organs. The red crickets are on his face. The hand around his heart squeezes until Ayson screams. The red crickets enter his mouth, his nose, and crawl into his ears. The First Etabli's final scream is silenced, his breath stolen.

His last thought is an image of Quel…the Adow… dying in his arms.

His heart is pulled from his chest, and Ayson dies.

Teyo mounts a charge to recover his body. The warriors stand in a circle, protecting the remains of the First Etabli from the Rorne.

Faunride tries valiantly to reach the Adow, but there are too many scholars. He is forced to protect himself.

All around them, the Adowian Army is being pushed back. The last warrior of the Abre 10th is killed. The Rovet of the Galesh 41st dies. The banner of the Stycral 38th is lowered. The Rorne continue to attack. Fear moves through the warriors as they witness the deaths of the strongest among them. Five warriors from the Mali 6th flee. Their Rovet sees them, spurs his horse, and runs them down with his spear. Then an eagle snatches his heart, and the Rovet falls from his horse.

Fifty-seven warriors from the Tesa 89th wield swords made by Hiate the blacksmith and Edran his apprentice. The Rorne die with each stroke of these swords, but the tribesmen fall back and continue their attack on the remainder of the army. They kill more than they lose. They bury their hands into the bodies of the warriors...and the taggles.

The taggles show no fear. The Rorne wrap their hands around their weakened hearts; barely pulsing–not like the heart of a warrior. Curious that such a creature has survived. Surely, the Sphere doesn't protect them, yet they live. It doesn't matter. The Rorne squeeze their hearts and they die.

The Tesa 89th attacks the right flank of the Rorne. When they joined the quest most of the warriors were without weapons. Now they carry the swords of Hiate, the blacksmith. The steel of Caduum rips through the Rorne like a hatchet through a chicken's throat. The tribesmen fall. They die.

Hiate and Edran appear on the horizon and run their horses to the front of the battle. Hiate leaps from his horse into the Rorne, barreling into three scholars. The blacksmith rolls to his feet and sends his blade into two of the three, spearing both of them at once. He pulls it out and swings at the third whose head falls from his body. A hand reaches for Edran, but the apprentice severs it. He kills another, causing the Rorne to back away from him.

Hiate charges like a wild hog. He lowers his shoulder and crashes into the scholars. They fall to the ground. They die. He rolls and kills another. His thick legs are bent, enabling him to stay low. His balance gives him the advantage. He punches. He kicks. He buries his sword into them.

The Adowian Army rallies around the blacksmith.

~

The scholars enter the Adow's tent where Hintor stands ready to slay them. He charges with the steel of Caduum in his hands. Behind him, Nataline wraps DK Vel in her arms as though he were one of her daughters. She holds a knife in her hand, but more than anything she prays the Sphere will deliver her from this nightmare.

Hintor stalls the attack. Then he's gone, chasing the scholars outside the tent. Nataline calls after him, but there's no response—only the muffled sounds of battle. Something crashes against the tent behind them causing Nataline to turn with a start. Nothing there. A slumping shadow, probably a body. Another crash followed by the squawk of an eagle. The bird rips through the roof, falling in a disoriented heap ten feet from where DK Vel sits. Nataline wraps her hand around the bird's head and lops it off with the oft-practiced skill of a cook. Then she cowers as the eagle transforms into the severed body of a scholar.

Hintor returns, takes a quick assessment of the scene, and grins. "Not much for conversation, are they?"

"Where were you!" Nataline yells.

But Hintor doesn't have time to answer. Two more scholars enter the tent. Again Nataline wraps her arms around the taggle boy while they watch Hintor beat back the assault.

~

Inindu looks out across the battlefield. There is an odd silence to the battle. The warriors shout commands. Eagles squawk. And the screams...yet everything feels muted. The Rorne have no weapons, so there is no clashing of swords.

A tiger roars as it leaps toward Teyo. The warrior's head strikes the ground with a ferocious thud. The tiger licks his unconscious face, all but removing the helmet as his tongue moves up Teyo's head. He pulls back and bites into the warrior's throat. Teyo quivers and dies.

The tiger looks toward Inindu, nestling close to the ground. It charges and leaps, but Inindu's hair wraps around the beast. It struggles at first to free itself from her grip, but the tiger grows calm, slowly relaxing until it is completely still. Inindu unwinds her hair. The body is gone. She reaches for another scholar.

Then the sky ignites with fire—scattering and killing the eagles.

The Kul has arrived.

"'Tis a poor place for a creature of such beauty."

Inindu turns at the familiar voice. Hiate the blacksmith walks up behind her, followed by his apprentice. "Perhaps you'll lead me to a better place, Hiate of Caduum."

Hiate buries his sword in a tribesman's chest; yanks it out. "'Tis the Adow I've come to rescue, no offense meant to yerself."

"Then I will leave you to your purpose, Hiate of Caduum."

"And I to yers." The blacksmith glances at the sky—at the Kul. "Daughter…" He suddenly grins. "…may the Sphere be with you."

"Maldinado would be a much more useful companion." Inindu lowers her head, slightly. "No offense."

Hiate bows. "None taken." Blacksmith and apprentice leave Inindu and travel toward the flaming sword of the Adow.

Inindu reaches for another scholar even as she watches Morlac's greatest creation descend from the sky. The Kul is a yearling consumed by fire. Her pale white skin appears and disappears from behind the flames. She has black hair and thin violet lips. But she has no eyes. That's always bothered Inindu. And the swollen eyes of the scholars; they've always bothered her, too, as though they offered their eyes in sacrifice to their blind god.

"Fools!"

Chad Michael Cox

The scholars bow before the Kul as it lands on the battlefield. Inindu has never felt inclined to bow to anyone, nor is she prone to fear. She gallops toward the Kul without another thought.

Behind her, Hiate and his apprentice reach the Adow. She is staring at the Kul with a madness that reveals her thoughts. "You can't be defeating it, my Adow."

The Adow turns on the blacksmith with a fire that matches the flames of her sword. "I won't flee."

"You must flee." Hiate continues undiscouraged. "I won't allow you to be dying on the battlefield like yer mother. Let yer warriors fight for you. Let them die with the honor they seek!"

"I won't leave my warriors!"

"Ovda, you can't be winning this battle." Hiate responds.

"What did you call me?" The Adow's flaming sword is suddenly extinguished.

"An old friend of yers asked me to watch after you. 'Tis a warrior named Troq."

"My Adow!" Faunride comes running to her side, pushing past Hiate and his apprentice. "My Adow, the First Etabli is dead."

Edran motions toward the battlefield. "Master, she's there."

Faunride turns to see Inindu, "What is she doing?"

"'Tis her purpose to be facing the dark creature," Hiate explains.

The Adow cannot take her eyes off the blacksmith. "You knew Troq?"

Hiate doesn't respond. His attention is focused solely on the scene in the distance, two champions facing one another. But that alone isn't what draws his attention. He is waiting for something else to happen, first.

God of Another World: The Adow

Inindu doesn't slow down. There's no sense in delaying the proceedings, so she charges toward the Kul without concern for ceremony.

Maldinado appears in front of her, unexpectedly forcing Inindu to come to a halt beside him. "The Adarian 45th requests the honor of being the first to attack this creature."

"Protect your Adow, Madar!"

"I won't run away."

"This isn't your fight!" Inindu moves to stop him. "Protect your Adow!"

"The honor is ours!" Maldinado tries to get around Inindu, but she easily matches his movements.

"And what of your sister?" Inindu changes tactics. "Who will protect her?"

Maldinado doesn't move.

"Damn your sense of honor!" Then a thought occurs to her. She looks back toward the elevated spot where she left her father. The red beard of the blacksmith is just visible in the distance. "He wouldn't..." But she knows he has… she told him she would rather take Maldinado over the Sphere…and here he stands.

And why shouldn't Maldinado be with her? The Adow stole Adarian from her, took her lover without so much as a whispered apology. Beyond that, her sister is a fool. She would choose Maldinado to be her First Etabli instead of Faunride, repeating the cycle her mother began. Her choice would bring about another Quel. Yes, *this* is the will of the Sphere…so let it be done.

"Very well, Madar. You will have your wish, but we fight the Kul together." Inindu turns back toward Maldinado. "Take my hand."

He climbs onto the magenta horse to sit behind the

magenta-haired topi, and wraps his arms around her slender waist.

"Do you know why we burn our dead?" Inindu charges the Kul, traveling faster than any horse Maldinado has ever ridden.

"I've never thought much about it." He draws his sword, though he is uncertain what effect it will have on the creature, if any.

Inindu carries no weapon and, strangely, her hair is completely still. "Fire serves as a gateway to another world."

When they reach the Kul Inindu carries Maldinado directly into the fire, leaping without hesitation even as the Madar yells, "For Adarian!"

But the battle of champions is over too quickly. Inindu and Maldinado are both consumed by the Kul. They are gone.

~

"What is she doing?" The Adow watches in horror as Inindu charges the Kul. "Who's that with her?"

"'Tis a brave warrior to be certain."

They disappear into the Kul, blackness enveloping magenta.

"What happened? I can't see them." Faunride strains to see past the Kul, certain Inindu must have passed through the creature, but there is no sign of them.

"It was Maldinado..." The Adow answers her own question. "Both of them...gone...because of me."

"Come, my Adow. We can't be waiting any longer." Hiate lowers his sword.

"My Adow?" Faunride turns his blade on the blacksmith. "Who are you?"

He bows. "Hiate, a blacksmith from Caduum."

God of Another World: The Adow

"Inindu told me I should meet you." The Adow mutters.

The Tesa 89th is the next to challenge the Kul. They, too, are consumed. The Stycral 16th is next. The Kiel 9th. They all die.

Hiate takes the reigns from Edran and mounts his horse. "It be time, Ovda." He extends his hand to the Adow who allows herself to be pulled onto the back of his horse. The blacksmith looks down at Faunride. "Yer welcome to ride with Edran, fine warrior. At least until we find more horses. I imagine there be some near the Adow's tent which happens to be our immediate destination."

The four of them ride west, away from the Kul, but not far enough to avoid the horrors of sight and sound. It is an endless succession of screams and consuming fire. Warriors die in massive numbers, incinerated while attacking–or fleeing. It doesn't matter. Everyone around the Kul is quickly gone.

The scholars resume their attack, bolstered by the victory of their champion. Hiate and Edran are forced to alter their course, but they do not stray from their destination. They reach the Adow's tent to find Hintor fighting back two more scholars. Faunride and Edran assist with the kills and emerge with an unharmed Hintor, Nataline, and DK Vel who grins at the site of Hiate.

"Get some horses." Hiate says. "It be time to leave."

"I won't leave without Maldinado." Hintor declares.

Nataline agrees.

"I'm afraid yer Madar be dead." Hiate informs them.

"Then it was him." The Adow confirms her own suspicions.

"They died with honor." Faunride says.

Nataline falls into Hintor's arms, unwilling to believe

her brother is dead. Hintor knew this day would come, but he is unprepared for the burden of emotion that threatens to break him. He buries his nose into Nataline's hair, fighting his own tears.

Hiate spurs his horse forward, the Adow still mounted behind him. "There be no time to mourn. Find yer horses and follow me. We've a quest 'tis needs our attention."

"No Hiate. No more lies." The Adow says as they ride away. "There is no quest. It was just a story that Troq told me when he was still alive." She buries her head into his back and starts to cry. "I just want to go home."

"The prophecy you told may be a lie, but the story be as true as my beard. There be five creatures in the Torment, alright. They've been waiting here a long time for someone to find them." Hiate pats the hand of the Adow around his waist. "I suppose it be about time we did just that."

THE ADOW

I'm awakened by a taggle.

"My Adow, come see." DK Vel whispers. He's a shadow in the darkness.

"What is it?" I climb out from under the blanket. Waiting for my eyes to adjust.

We made camp somewhere deep in the Torment. Hiate pushed the horses as hard as possible to get clear of the Rorne and Morlac's beast. I can only imagine what happened to the rest of the army we left behind to face the Kul. My greatest champions. Gone in an instant. What chance do we have to survive against such a creature? I look into the starless sky, searching for any sign of the eagles. Any sign of attack. Nothing.

DK Vel leads me slowly through a forest of balor trees. "What is it, taggle?"

He doesn't respond. Whatever it is has the boy excited.

I draw my sword.

The boy slows to a stop and I kneel beside him. "This is where Hiate disappeared." The boy says. "We were walking together, and then he was gone."

"What do you mean he's gone?"

"Gone. He was there, and then he wasn't. That's when I saw the light." He points into the distance ahead.

My sword erupts with fire even as my senses are heightened, suddenly fearful the boy has led me into an ambush–certain Hiate's body is lying butchered somewhere nearby. The sword serves as a torch, illuminating the forest around me. There's no sign of a struggle. Where did he go? I check the surrounding area, but there is nothing out of the ordinary. Only the light ahead, maybe a mile away.

I look back at the boy. Shadows and firelight flicker across his sallow face and sweaty torso. He's mostly naked. His black hair as tangled as mine. Why did he come for me? Hintor is his master. Does he presume to be mine now that Inindu is dead?

"Before he disappeared, Hiate told me to give you a message." The boy says, as though reading my mind. "He said you'll hear his voice in the stories."

I search again for the blacksmith, hoping to find his body. It feels like there should be a body, or some sign of his passing. Tasa Ro! "What kind of…" I don't even know what I want to say. Dammit!

"My Adow, was Hiate the Sphere?"

"Yes, boy." Yes, the Sphere is a red-bearded blacksmith from Caduum. Of course he is…and before that he was my guardian, my storyteller. Did my mother know? Has it always been this way with the Adow–is that how they communicated with the Sphere? Or is it the other way around–is that how the Sphere communicates with his Adow?

The boy points toward the light.

Yes, the light. I lead the boy through the trees, easily navigating the path with my flaming sword. He follows me like Ayson used to follow me. No sword, of course. He'll be useless if this turns out to be a fight. Then again, Ayson wouldn't be any better. And he's dead, anyway.

My father is dead.

And Inindu…and Maldinado.

I could use the Madar right about now. For a moment I consider returning to the camp, going back for Faunride and Hintor, but I push the thought away. I'm the one holding a flaming sword.

The light grows and separates as we move closer, several different lights without a source. They aren't torches, or I would see the warriors that hold them. In fact, there's no obvious explanation for the light. I search the surrounding area, but there is no one lying in wait. No sign of danger, yet.

We enter a large clearing and slowly move toward the closest sphere, drawn by curiosity. I touch it. I wrap my free hand around its smooth, warm surface. The sphere is vibrating with the energy that emanates from within. The light grows brighter, a blinding white that forces me to look away. The taggle falls prostrate behind me. Are taggles always this reverent?

The white light fades to a warm glow, allowing me to see a golden figure in place of the sphere. It's a sculpted image of a male yearling. An odd statue… The yearling's hair is like a splash in the pond at the moment of impact, a large curling wave suspended above his head. Another curl hangs over his right eye. The wildness of his hair reminds me of Inindu—less frightening but just as disturbing.

I leave the taggle to his worship and touch another sphere. Blinding light and golden figure, but this one is different. He's squinting; his eyelids seemingly heavier than what he can bear—burdens that bring age to his otherwise youthful features. I run my fingers over his golden face. It's warm, almost hot to the touch, the power within barely contained.

I touch the other three spheres. Three more golden figures. One with a furrowed brow. One with a face of great sadness. And the last…such innocence, his eyes wide with wonder. I touch his cheek and find it as hardened as the other figures. Golden statues. Why? Why are they here in the middle of the Torment? Are these the creatures Hiate said we would find? The wolves? Maybe the quest isn't a lie, but how? It was a story! I told a story and now here they are; five wolves. The five Arms of the Sphere–we found them.

A taggle found them.

DK Vel is peeking up from his prostrate position, his curiosity finally getting the better of his reverence.

"What was it Hiate told you to tell me?"

"You'll hear his voice in the stories."

"How many stories do you know, DK Vel?" How many stories did Troq tell me? Are they all filled with prophecies? Why didn't my mother or any of the other Adow tell me these stories?

"I've never counted."

A presence enters the clearing with such force that I'm thrown to the ground. The presence becomes a white sphere that forms in the middle of the circle of statues. Streams of light pierce the night, extending from the sphere into the Arms of the Sphere with such violence it sends sparks crackling through the darkness in a thousand directions. I see everything for a moment, the image forever frozen in my memory. Then I'm forced to shield my eyes.

Gusts of hot air beat against me. My ears are filled with a tremendous buzzing–vibrations of power I recognize from when I held the sphere. Is the boy feeling this? I can't see him, he must be frightened. I stand and look away from the light, blindly navigating my way around the clearing. I have to reach the boy. Is this what it's like to be a mother?

"DK!" Where is he? I can't find my storyteller, my connection to the Sphere.

"I'm here. I can't see."

I kneel beside him and wrap my arm around him, bury my face into his unwashed hair. Tasa Ro! He needs a bath, and some clothes. I turn my head away from his hair, away from the light. "It's alright. You're going to be alright." I hold my sword at the ready, searching the darkness for any surprise.

"It's him, isn't it? The Sphere?"

"Yes, boy. I think it is."

Then the light is gone. The presence disappears from the clearing, and we're left with only the fire from my sword.

A soft voice calls out from behind us, "Mother?"

"Who's there?" I stand to face the threat.

A single flame appears, held above someone's hand. Five yearlings stand before us, golden figures come to life. The one holding the flame is the second figure that appeared, the one who was–who *is* squinting. I was right about the power inside of him.

"Their taggles." DK Vel notices.

I look at their ears. He's right. The five wolves are taggle boys.

The flame disappears as Faunride crashes into the clearing. "My Adow! The scholars have found us!"

Chad Michael Cox

Hintor, Nataline, and Edran emerge behind him leading the horses.

"I'm just glad we decided to forego the campfire tonight." Hintor deadpans. "Wouldn't want them to know where we're at."

An eagle squawks overhead.

a taggle's tale

As spoken by the Adow.

"No more running." The Adow's sword flares with renewed life. She is flanked by Faunride.

Hintor smiles at the Adow's weapon. "It's tradition in Adarian to exchange swords before a battle."

"Not now, Hintor!" Nataline scolds.

Hintor shrugs and pulls his own sword.

Behind them, forgotten in the midst of a threat, Edran gathers the other six taggle boys to him. He stands as their sole protector, sword in hand.

The attack is furious. Horses scatter as the eagles invade, feathers flapping with rage. Sound becomes a deafening rush, a wave of pressure that drowns out the higher pitched, collective squawk.

Flames from the Adow's sword leap into the sky, splintering like lightning, moving from one bird to another, searing eagles faster than they can descend. Their bodies fall uncouthly, but there are too many. Several break through, more, and then more–thousands of them billow over the fire as though a waterfall obliterating the pathetic flame of a candle.

Faunride turns from the approaching assault to his Adow. *Her sword is not enough!* He takes her to the ground, shielding her with his own body.

The light from the Adow's sword is extinguished, leaving them all in complete darkness, enhancing the already deafening noise. The Adow shouts at Faunride, but what she says is lost in the confusion of the attack.

Hintor feels a rush of eagles fly past his face, a cold wind with the scent of decay. He swings his sword in blindness, mutters unheard quips. His clumsy sword connects with a thud, but the unexpected victim causes his sword to change course. The eagle, now dead, transforms into a scholar and the sudden shift in weight throws Hintor off-balance. He follows the Rorne tribesman to the ground, but he quickly recovers, pulling his sword from the body to swing in a wide arch. He strikes nothing.

The Adow's sword ignites anew. Faunride still covers her with his body, but she has managed to free her arm, raising the sword to the heavens. The sky is a mass of birds. Nothing exists beyond their piercing eyes, their yellow beaks.

"Get off me!" The Adow struggles against Faunride's grip, her rage matching the flames of her sword.

Faunride cannot help but focus on those flames. They no longer crackle from bird to bird like lighting in the sky. Now the fire is a singular pillar that rips through the assault. Faunride realizes she is their only hope. Finally, he releases his Adow.

She stands to fully absorb the attack, but the descending flood parts before the flames. The birds swoop away and return to the sky, so Faunride and Hintor move to the perimeter where the eagles are at their lowest point. They hack away and send the birds flailing into the darkness of the forest beyond, bodies transforming into tribesman as they fall.

The flames from the Sword of the Adow abruptly leap onto the blades of Faunride and Hintor. Then Nataline's, and even Edran's who points his Caduum forged weapon toward the flames as though calling them forth, inviting them. His face shows no surprise, a stark contrast to the expressions of Faunride, Hintor, and Nataline.

Five pillars of flame ignite the sky. The birds are incinerated, their charred remains turning to ash before they can transform. Hintor swings with unhindered power. *If Maldinado could see me now!* Nataline simply holds her blade aloft, unconsciously reaching out with her other hand to touch the head of the taggle around her leg, DK Vel. Behind her, Edran protects the remaining taggles.

Hundreds perish. Thousands remain. They circle and swarm, squawking without ceasing. They are everywhere; appearing and disappearing behind, through, and around strokes of flame that linger in the night. Again, Faunride worries that there are too many. The five swords of fire are not enough. He retreats to his Adow, ready to protect her once more; fully aware he will not rise again once he takes her to the ground. He will die as he was meant to die, as Maldinado died, while protecting his Adow.

Then the eagles fly away. They flee into the night, the rush of wind, along with their deafening squawks, fade to silence. Absent a threat, the fire from the five swords slowly diminishes, giving way to darkness.

Hintor's ears are ringing. His pupils widen as adrenaline

continues to fuel his body. "Run, you bastards!"

"No, look!" Faunride points to a red glow emerging above the trees. "The Kul approaches."

"Let it come!" The Adow spits the words, her sword flaring in response.

One of the taggles, Madic Baltin, steps away from the others, his eyes heavy with burden behind the rekindled flame above his outstretched hand. "Get behind me!"

The Adow looks at the forgotten taggle, stunned by his brashness, struggling to remember what occurred before the battle.

"Learn your place, taggle!" Faunride commands.

"Who are you?" Hintor sees the new taggle for the first time. "And who are they?" He points to the four boys huddled around Edran.

"They are the Arms of the Sphere." Edran says.

"The five wolves." The Adow remembers.

"Taggles?" Faunride turns to his Adow in alarm.

"Yes, taggles." She replies.

"*This* was our quest?" Hintor asks no one in particular. Then he erupts in rage. "Maldinado died for a bunch of taggles?"

"Hintor!" Nataline warns, but she cannot suppress her own feelings, suddenly aware of the taggle around her leg. "Don't touch me!"

DK Vel releases her leg and quickly, silently, rejoins the other boys.

The flame above Madic Baltin's hand grows larger.

"How is he doing that?" Faunride asks.

"I don't know." The Adow turns back toward the approaching Kul. "It doesn't matter. Nataline, get them out of here."

"My Adow?" Nataline doesn't move. "They're taggles."

God of Another World: The Adow

"I'm not leaving." Madic moves determinedly, brushing past the Adow until he is standing in front of her. "This is my purpose."

Faunride reacts to the obvious slight, bringing his sword down upon the offending taggle, but Madic raises his free hand in lackluster response. The sword, at the moment of contact with the taggle's hand, fragments into droplets of water that burst outward with harmless force.

Faunride stares at his hands. Everyone else is staring at Madic.

"My Adow." Edran breaks the silence. "You'll not be defeating the Kul with yer sword. 'Tis Madic's task to be certain."

The Adow doesn't retreat.

In fact, no one moves, for the Kul appears above them. The shadows are lost against the night sky leaving only a furious fire to define the creature. It's vast, a mass of swirling flame that fills the darkened horizon.

Hintor moves to wrap his arms around Nataline. "Don't look." He holds her head against his shoulder.

"Run!" Nataline whispers.

Hintor chuckles at the suggestion.

Nataline pushes off until she is looking him in the eye. "Take me to Plenrid. I want to be a farmer's wife."

The eagles return, made bold by the arrival of their champion. They flutter around, circle above, and finally populate the trees in the surrounding forest, seeking the best vantage point from which to view the final battle.

Hintor shakes his head. "No, Nataline. I may have been born in Plenrid, but I'll die an Adarian. Your brother made sure of that."

"You're not Adarian!"

"The unbroken circle on my chest says different."

Nataline smiles despite her fear. Both emotions highlighted by the flames of the Kul, now fully arrived overhead. "In that case, I'll marry you."

Hintor stares in befuddlement.

Nataline leans forward and kisses his uncertain lips, her tears wet against his nose. He drops his sword, wraps his arms around her, and awaits the Kul.

The creature draws closer. Eagles squawk and jostle amongst the leaves with anticipation. Faunride can feel the immense heat upon his body. His empty hands. They are clearly visible in the light of the Kul. And the creature before him, the taggle boy…or something else.

~

I am drawn to these taggles as though I truly am their mother, but I did not create them. They are a creation of the Sphere. I touched them, nothing more.

I look up toward the Kul. The final image of Inindu and Maldinado fills my mind, their bodies consumed by fire. Will I fair any better? I adjust my grip upon the sword—so much power. Is it enough? No, it isn't. Edran is right. We won't survive.

A taggle wraps himself around my leg, seeking my protection just as he did earlier tonight when the Sphere entered the clearing. It seems like a lifetime ago. I reach down to embrace his head. My storyteller. My link to the Sphere. *I wish I could've heard all of your stories, boy. I wish my daughter could've heard your stories.* "It's alright, DK. Everything will be alright."

No, not everything. One more act before we die. "Faunride!" He's still staring at Madic. *I don't have to do this. I can protect myself.* My sword flickers. "Faunride!" My protector finally turns. His eyes showing the devastation he feels at being so humiliated. *Yes, I have to do this…it's what*

God of Another World: The Adow

he needs. I extend my sword, inviting him to take it. "I'm in need of a First Etabli."

He hesitates for only a moment. I can't blame him. The Kul, Madic, squawking eagles…it's a lot to absorb. Then, with a familiar gait, his right foot turned slightly inward, he hastens to my side and takes my sword. The flames go out the moment my hand leaves the hilt. *Well, that's a little disappointing.* It doesn't matter. It isn't about the sword. I saw the hurt in Faunride's eyes during the Greeting Rituals, when I didn't choose him to ride to Adarian. I won't do that again. He deserves this honor…he's always been there for me.

I kneel down beside DK Vel and hold him to my throat as the Kul draws closer. "I'm here, boy. Everything will be alright."

Faunride stands beside me, his leg against my back. Yes, Faunride, you may touch me. Yes, you may die for me.

~

Madic Baltin waits for the Kul with the patience of a fisherman. Though, certainly, the creature is only moments from consuming them all: the Adow, Faunride and DK Vel; Hintor and Nataline; and Edran who is surrounded by the golden-robed, remaining Arms of the Sphere. Madic's brothers.

Beads of perspiration run down the side of his face. With his free hand Madic brushes the sweat into his unkempt hair, making it slick around his ears. With his other hand he raises the flame, allowing it to expand upward toward the Kul, toward the face without eyes. The creature continues downward, she is unaware, or unconcerned with the taggle's flame.

Madic's unwavering flame stretches until it is touching the fire of the Kul, sliding into her like a fisherman's hook. The Kul stops, aware of the foreign presence–one it cannot consume. Madic's flame begins to retract, drawing down the flames of the Kul. Like a net pulling fish from the sea, Madic pulls fire down out of shadow. The creature howls with a vicious wind, striking at the source of her pain—the taggle below, but the boy continues to gather and pull fire from the Kul.

There is no more squawking. The eagles watch with cocked heads as their champion is drained of its most terrifying threat.

And then the fire is gone.

All that remains is Madic's small flame suspended above his palm. He lowers his hand and the flame disappears.

Above them, the Kul rages like a wounded animal. She strikes quickly, defensively, consuming the taggle and his companions, burying them in shadow and chaos. Faunride swings the Adow's sword, but he finds nothing to strike. The wind is warm, even hot upon his face. Sound is buffered. Breath is taken. Shadow is everything. The newly appointed First Etabli understands. He lowers his sword, and embraces his death.

It never comes.

Madic Baltin stands with his feet slightly spread, his arms extending downward at an angle, hands open. His eyes widen against the wind, causing tears to form and stream backward toward his ears. He opens his mouth and tastes the darkness.

Then he devours it.

The Kul swirls and funnels into the taggle's mouth, a maelstrom with Madic at its center. The face without eyes floats helplessly through waves of darkness and shadow, her pale skin is swept under the current only to emerge once more, always encircling her captor. The formlessness of shadow and wind gather toward a single point below where Madic consumes, spreading his feet a little wider as the Kul enters his body. Her body is completely absorbed.

Madic closes his mouth.

Squawk. It's an unseen eagle amidst thousands still watching from the trees.

Madic turns his head toward the sound and opens his mouth. Then he erupts. His body explodes—a bright light quickly overwhelmed by the darkness of the Kul within, no longer contained. The force throws everyone to the ground except Edran. He remains unaffected.

DK Vel opens his eyes. The Adow still clings to him, but he can see past her arms, now. Where the trees once stood, full of eagles, there is nothing but dirt, extending the perimeter of the clearing by several hundred yards. And there, surrounding him and his companions completely, is a barrier of fire…and shadow. And wind. It is the Kul. The barrier extends overhead so that they are fully enclosed within a sphere.

"There be nothing more to fear." Edran says.

"What happened?" Faunride asks.

The Adow stands undaunted, lifting DK Vel whom she embraces at her side. "Are we inside the Kul?"

"No." Edran says. "The Kul be existing in a different form. Her purpose was altered."

"And the boy?" The Adow looks around.

"Madic's purpose 'tis fulfilled. My master created him to protect his brothers."

Hintor turns toward the remaining Arms of the Sphere. They are huddled around Edran; taggles of varying heights and features. Their expressions range from unreadable to a look of terror, but they are nothing so unfamiliar. He has seen similar expressions from taggles, before. Certainly, there is nothing to suggest they are worth the sacrifice of so many, yet their power is undeniable…even frightening.

"Where is your master?" The Adow asks Edran.

"'Tis a fair question to be certain. Perhaps he be waiting on the other side of the Kul." Edran begins to walk. "'Tis time we be leaving this place."

Edran walks without concern. Neither does he pause before disappearing behind the wall of fire and shadow. A moment later, he reappears.

"'Tis nothing to fear, my Adow. Walk quickly through the Kul and you'll suffer no harm." Again Edran moves in and out of the Kul. "Do not linger, though, or the Kul be consuming you same as it ever did."

Edran disappears behind the Kul.

Hintor looks around. "Who's next?" No one moves. "Tasa Ro! Why does the Adarian 45th always have to lead?" He retrieves his sword, gives Nataline a kiss, and enters the Kul.

His body feels the weight of the Kul immediately, pulling his skin downward as though peeling it from the top of his skull. His eyes close under the force, and his lungs struggle to gather air around his tongue which falls to the back of his throat. His stomach collapses inward, legs waver. He can barely keep hold of his sword.

It is only a moment, for Hintor emerges from the Kul as though swimming to the surface of a lake. He desperately inhales the forest air then exhales with disgust. His mouth tastes like smoke, his tongue numb as though burned. He searches for Edran, but the taggle is nowhere to be found. Hintor calibrates himself. He's in the forest, but there is no sign of the eagles. It's dark, but the Kul provides more than enough light. There are two walls of fire and shadow on either side of him. They extend outward from the circle he just passed through into the forest and out of sight.

"Tasa Ro! How big is this thing?"

~

I can't sleep. The walls of the Kul on either side of me feel like a cage, so I sit with my back against a balor tree, resisting the urge to flee. Faunride, still holding my sword, stands guard above me as my newly appointed First Etabli. He stares at the Kul as though waiting for it to strike. Despite what Edran said, I can't help but wonder if we really *are* inside the creature. *Are you here, Maldinado? Inindu?* But our camp was exactly the same when we returned. Except now we are flanked on either side by the Kul.

I can tell the others feel the same apprehension. Hintor stares out into the darkness, sword raised, holding Nataline's hand same as he has since we emerged from the Kul. If we have emerged. The Arms of the Sphere are huddled together in silence. I'm not sure what to say to them. Madic Baltin seemed so sure of himself. These four just seem lost; newborns attempting to stand.

I run my fingers through DK Vel's hair, his head resting against my leg.

"Will we ever see Edran, again?" The taggle asks.

"I don't know." The blacksmith's apprentice vanished without a trace. We searched for him, moving through the Kul several times. *Not a pleasant experience!* But we didn't find him.

"Or the Sphere?"

"The Sphere is always with us, boy." I know that now.

"Do they have the same powers as the other taggle had?"

I look again at the remaining Arms of the Sphere. They are a complete mystery to me. "Did Hiate tell you anything about them?" The boy shakes his head against my leg. "Then I think there is much I must learn about taggles."

DK Vel suddenly sits up, causing Faunride and Hintor to react with alarm. But the taggle isn't afraid. He didn't see something in the distance. He's staring right at me, excited.

"Tasa Ro!" Hintor curses.

"What is it boy?" I ask.

"I found them. I led you right to the Arms of the Sphere. That means I get an Adowian Burial!"

"Yes, boy, you will receive an Adowian Burial when you die." Even as I say it I realize what I have done. The taggles will never be the same.

DK Vel smiles and returns to where he was laying against my leg.

He sits up again, bringing another reaction from Faunride and Hintor.

"Learn your place, taggle!" Faunride steps forward. The taggle cowers in reaction.

I hold up my hand to keep my First Etabli from killing the boy. "His place is with me, Faunride." I grab the back of the taggle's head and bring him to me. "Are you always this restless?"

"I just realized…Madic Baltin…" The boy's fear gives way to renewed enthusiasm. "He didn't really die. A taggle saved the Adow! That story will be told forever!"

Dsal Tiger

This tale originated in Yenul, a bedtime story told by my guardian, Troq, whom I now know was embodied by the Sphere as was Hiate after him. Troq's dark hands held me close to his heart and I could feel his white beard against my head. He told me many stories about Tiger, which I later discovered was the same tiger as the one described by the taggles as Dsal Tiger. I always imagined Troq's tiger to be white with black stripes, similar to my guardian. This was the first story he told me, the one he told me most often.

His tale, the Sphere's tale, began: Listen to my story, Ovda, and may my words forever guide you.

— The Adow

Tiger walks through a valley in Dragon's Torment where he has tracked the five wolves. Many have sought the wolves and never returned.

The bear is dead.

The lion is lost.

The owl has fled.

But Tiger remains. He looks around. Sniffs the air. Continues carelessly, loudly, breaking sticks as he walks.

The sound echoes throughout the valley.

A falcon hears the noise from overhead. "Flee this valley," it shrieks. "The Kul approaches."

"Have you seen the wolves?" Tiger calls, but the falcon flies away without another word.

Tiger doesn't flee. He's thirsty. The rain taunts him from a distance. He seeks a river, a lake–dew drops suspended from leaves, but there is nothing to quench his thirst. Finally, at the top of a mountain, above timberline, he finds a lake. He runs to its edge, lowering his head to drink. The water is cold as it travels through his body.

A fish appears, a small ripple within the waves created by Tiger's insatiable lapping. "Run from these waters. The Kul approaches."

"Have you seen the wolves?" Tiger asks, water dripping from the white fur around his mouth, but the fish is gone.

Tiger doesn't run. He's tired. He moves deeper into the Torment in search of a comfortable spot to rest, eventually coming upon a cave. He curls up, falls asleep beside a large rock.

The cave is filled with bats. "Leave this cave," they squeak. "The Kul approaches."

Tiger awakens to the sound of bats leaving the cave. "Have you seen the wolves?" he asks sleepily, but none of the bats turn at his question, so Tiger resumes his slumber.

There is the roar of a bear.

And the roar of a lion.

But neither bear nor lion appear. Their roars echo from within the Kul, a creature of wind and shadow–a creature now standing at the mouth of the cave. The Kul has come!

Tiger is awake.

The roar of the bear fades. And that of the lion.

Another sound, barely perceptible, is all that remains of the owl. "Who?"

Tiger feels the fur on his spine rise. He growls at the Kul, raises his paw in warning. The Kul is undeterred. Tiger lunges with a roar, but the creature of wind and shadow consumes him. He is gone, a lingering echo from within the Kul.

ABOUT THE AUTHOR

CHAD MICHAEL COX is an award winning author and freelance writer whose work has appeared in numerous publications since graduating from the writing program at Emerson College in Boston, MA. He spent his youth at the foot of the Rocky Mountains in Colorado, and now lives in Iowa with his wife and three children.